ALSO BY TIM MEYER

NOVELS

In the House of Mirrors
The Thin Veil
Less Than Human
Sharkwater Beach
Primal Terra
Lords of the Deep (with Patrick Lacey)
The Switch House
Kill Hill Carnage
Limbs
69
Dead Daughters
Malignant Summer (coming soon)

DEMON BLOOD SERIES

Enlightenment
Gateways
Defiance

COLLECTIONS

Worlds Between My Teeth
Black Star Constellations

THE SWITCH HOUSE

TIM MEYER

EVIL EPOCH
PRESS

THE SWITCH HOUSE
Hardcover Edition: 2020
Copyright © 2020 by Tim Meyer
Edited by Jenny Adams
ISBN: 978-1732399358

Cover design by Don Noble | roosterrepublicpress.com
Interior design by Todd Keisling | Dullington Design Co.
Interior illustrations by James "Toe" Keen

Published by Evil Epoch Press
Printed in the United States of America

EVIL EPOCH
PRESS

For Ashley,
This one is yours. Sort of.

THE SWITCH HOUSE

"Still she haunts me, phantomwise,
Alice moving under skies
Never seen by waking eyes."
—Lewis Carroll, *Through the Looking-Glass and What Alice Found There*

*T*he house stands in the middle of the dirt road, the nexus of Everywhere. Overhead, the skies roll in a spreading blanket of tumbling fog. The sun hides somewhere beyond, however, the gray lid makes it impossible for significant light to appear. A shadowy shield buries this place, this vast emptiness of nonexistence.

The house stands on a property belonging to no one. The property consists of a front lawn, a backyard, a stockade fence stained the color of dead autumn leaves and a deluxe swing-set showing little wear. The windows remain intact, the marine-blue vinyl siding rests in perfect condition, the shutters expertly hung, darkly colored to accent the blue. The roof, no less than a year old, is free from mildew stains. Where the property ends lies a colorless wasteland, an endless lot of desolation filled with dirt and gravel, and if anyone was to dig beneath the empty plots, they might discover a skeleton or two.

Or twelve.

Or a thousand.

Impossible to tell how many souls have wandered this endless place. Come to live, leave to die.

The house is a tomb. Not her tomb. Not yet. But a tomb nonetheless.

She walks up the stoop and approaches the front door, the blood-red barrier between the cool atmosphere grazing her exposed arms and legs and the fireplace-heated interior, which will warm her from the inside out. She slips the key into the lock and pushes the door open.

Who gave me the key? *she asks the dream's absent architect.*

Access resides within you, child, *an omnipotent voice replies, supplying her* veins with ice. No matter how warm and cozy the inside of the house may be, she thinks she'll never shake that frigid feeling from her bones. The brisk sensation clings to her, infiltrates her pores and nests in her marrow.

She decides to keep her questions to herself from here on out, though, in this place, in this Everywhere, the rules are different and she doubts her mind will remain silent, even if that's her wish. And, of course, another presence lurks behind her, invisible and almighty. The phantom has followed her up the stoop, through the front door and into the living room.

It breathes in her ear.

She spins.

Nothing there but the open doorway and the barren wasteland yonder. She stares at the entryway as the exterior landscape warps and twists, the image swirling like toilet water. After the desolate, ashen world of perpetual ruin melts away, the view fades, embodies a starry black expanse. She realizes she's looking the elements of space and time in the face and her mind feels like a cheap piece of glass ready to break, ready to crumble, ready to cut and draw blood.

She blinks and discovers the door has shut itself, turning the black nothingness away, the prospect of eternal madness temporarily kept at bay.

She faces the living room. The house appears differently than its real-life counterpart. In real life, lilac walls hold up the ceiling and a wrought-iron table stands by the stairs, displaying a fresh bouquet of either roses or violet pansies. In real life, the floors are always swept and polished, so much so that guests marvel over their crisp reflections. In real life, the plush leather couch faces an eighty-inch television screen, mint as the day it was manufactured. Here, now, in the middle of the Everywhere, the house's interior décor lies in havoc. The couch is ripped and torn, tossed before a television screen appearing to have been smashed by a mallet, a mess of wires hanging from its open face like a mouthful of electric spaghetti noodles. The vase near the stairs holds dead black flowers, wilted and filling the air with stomach-churning fragrances reminding her of rancid meat. The floors have been scratched and muddied with bootprints. The walls are no longer lilac; in fact, they hold no color. And they're moving. Not moving in one direction or the other, not gliding, but writhing.

Crawling. Wriggling. Squirming.

It takes her a moment to realize the walls are alive, pulsing with maggots.

But it's not just the walls that are alive; the house itself is alive and she hears the drum of its heartbeat along with her own.

She watches herself walk. Toward the kitchen. She hears footsteps ahead of her and stops. She's waiting for something to happen, waiting for the omnipotent driver of this dream to steer her in new directions. That, or she's waiting for the architect to grant her access to her own bodily functions so she can run, run like hell, run like the devil's chasing her.

Because he is.

He's over her shoulder, whispering thoughts. Sharing intrusive images. Marking her. Prepping her permanent residence in the belly of Everywhere-land.

The devil.

Well, not the actual devil. But something like him, something that schemes with nefarious intentions, that lures, beckons her deeper into hell with a long, taloned finger.

Some unnamed thing.

The shuffling grows louder. She stays frozen, her feet stuck to the urethane-coated floor, feeling like a fly in a spider web.

And the spider is coming.

A small thing appears in the doorway separating the living room and the kitchen, a shadow belonging to a small boy; a tiny boy; a little baby boy. Older now than when she last saw him. He's covered in mud, dripping with shadows and some clear viscous slop that reminds her of embryonic fluid. Through the shade and the sludge coating his flesh, she sees the whites of his eyes, the stark brightness of his baby teeth. She can't tell but she thinks he's smiling. Such a good boy. A nice boy. A happy boy.

"Ma-me," the boy says, but as he speaks she notices differences, specifically the throaty gargle deepening his voice. No, not a boy. A thing. A predatory thing hiding beneath the flesh of an innocent child, an unseen monstrosity that growls instead of articulating, a thing that gnashes its teeth when silent. "Ma-me," the thing that is not a boy says once more.

Shivers curl around her spine. She chokes on the foul air, polluted by the boy-thing's earthly odor. The thing steps forward.

Closer.

And closer.

And...

The thing stands before her, inches from her face. He's floating, lying on an invisible magic carpet. They're eye to eye now, locked in an epic battle of who-blinks-first. She stares into the monster's snow-white eyes as they grow darker and darker until she finds herself gazing into another starry black nothingness; one harboring hatred and rage; one craving violence and the sweet taste of death.

She peers into the Everywhere, gets lost, and drifts away...

"Ma-me," it says with a growl and, this time, a painful bite.

I.

WELCOME HOME, ANGELA SHEPARD

Well, what do *you* think it means?"

Her psychiatrist had been in the middle of scribbling something on her yellow legal pad, but now her pen hovered over the paper. She eyed Angela over her glasses, the way a schoolteacher awaits an explanation of missing homework. *She wants more,* Angela thought. But there was nothing more. She had told her everything, every single detail.

"Quite a dream," Abbie Wilson replied, resting her pad and pen down on her lap. "Did these dreams start after the tragedy?"

The tragedy. Angela hated the way that sounded. She wished Abbie could reference what happened differently, but she couldn't come up with anything better herself, so…

"Yes. But not like this. They stopped altogether when we were on *Switch.* Didn't have a single nightmare while shooting."

Abbie nodded, and then scooped up her pad and pen like she had suddenly remembered something important and pertinent. Hastily, she scribbled down her thoughts. "Let's talk about *Switch.*"

"Okay."

"You've been back from Vermont for how long now? Two days?"

Angela squinted, trying to recall. The return home had felt like an eternity ago, but yes, Abbie was correct. They'd left Vermont and crossed the New York/New Jersey border just under forty-eight hours ago. "Yes. But

God, it feels like years ago." She felt a manic laugh creep into her throat but swallowed the outburst before the noise seized the opportunity to launch past her teeth.

Abbie offered a faint smile. "Yes, time seems to work differently on those who have a lot on their mind. How does it feel being back home?"

Angela shuddered, a chill in the room diving beneath her flesh. "It feels... different. But the same. Like I never left, but simultaneously, like I was never there to begin with. I know that makes absolutely no sense, but—"

"No, it does," the woman assured her. She adjusted her glasses. "I'm sorry. Please continue."

"But I feel... jumbled. Out of place. Like the house is a puzzle and I'm the final piece that doesn't fit no matter how you spin me."

"That's an interesting metaphor."

Angela jerked her shoulders. "It's how I feel."

"Like a stranger in a familiar house?"

"Yes, I guess that's another way of putting it."

"How's Terry taking the adjustment?"

Angela paused. She wondered about Terry. *Worried,* she thought, was more like it. *You worry about Terry.* He had left work about the same time as the start of her session and would be home by now. "Eh, you know Terry. If something's wrong, you'll never hear about it."

"Has he gotten any better? I mean, when the two of you were on *Switch,* did he ever open up for the cameras? Speak his mind? Tell you how he felt? That was one of the goals you wanted to work on."

"He did. Sort of. The cameras on us twenty-four-seven definitely helped. I mean, he *had* to be open. We *had* to discuss things. That's what we signed up for. It was in our contract."

"Was he candid?"

Angela thought back to a few weeks ago when the producer of *Let's Switch Houses!,* Barry Harrison, pulled her aside and told her the Shepards were becoming a bit of a snoozefest, that they needed to produce some good material, quality footage, and fast, implying television ratings would surely dip if something interesting didn't happen and soon. Barry begged her to quiz Terry on "the tragedy." She doubted that conversation would go over well and, as it turned out, she had been right.

"Not as candid as the producers would have liked."

Abbie nodded and recorded her response. "And how did it make you feel?"

"Like we weren't… on the same team. God, I wish he'd just talk about it. I mean, it's been almost eight months."

"Must be frustrating." Abbie swallowed. "Angela, might I suggest we try to bring Terry in. For a couple's session."

Angela shook her head. "No, I told you. I don't want my husband to know I'm here."

"I can pretend it's the first time we've ever met. He won't even suspect—"

"No, Dr. Wilson. Absolutely not. He doesn't… he doesn't believe in this stuff. He thinks he's tougher than that. That he can deal with these emotions, these feelings, on his own. He doesn't want help." An intense burn seared her eyeballs. "I mean, he won't even talk to *me* for Christ's sakes."

"What do *you* think about it? Do you think he would benefit from therapy?"

Angela twisted her neck and focused on the walls, the hanging abstract art. "I don't know. Honestly, I don't know anything anymore."

"You didn't want to come home, did you, Angela?"

Tears set fire behind her eyes, and she pinched her eyelids shut to keep her face dry. "No, not really. I hate that house. I hate everything about it."

"Has the realtor helped any?"

She shook her head. "No. She says, because of… of what happened, we'd have to basically *give* away the house."

"That's a tough thing to hear," Abbie said, handing her a tissue. Angela sensed sincerity in her voice.

"Thank you." She blotted away the last of her tears. "We simply can't afford it. We can't afford to take a loss."

"I understand."

"I feel stuck."

Abbie tapped her pen on the pad. "None of this is your fault."

"Of course it is. If I—"

Abbie raised her hand. "Don't. Don't push the blame on yourself. We've talked about this, Angela, there's no need for self-accusations. What happened eight months ago was no one's fault. This is something you need to work on. Understand? Pushing blame on yourself isn't healthy, and furthermore, it's a lie. You did nothing wrong. The authorities cleared you of any potential charges and no one in the D.A.'s office batted an eye."

Angela nodded. Blame weighed heavily on her conscience, dragging her down like an anchor. She felt the pressure of the event *(the tragedy)* in her frontal lobe daily, an intense bass drum-like beat no over-the-counter prescription could erase.

Abbie sighed. "We have one more thing to talk about before our hour is up."

"Oh? I can't wait."

"Sex."

Oh. That. "Well, that's an easy one, Doc."

"Oh?"

"Yep. There isn't any. End of story."

Abbie looked like she wanted to laugh; however, the psychiatrist managed to keep her professional demeanor. "Did you and Terry try?" she asked. "During filming?"

"Yes," she said, recalling the three instances where they had tried to make love. "It was…"

(Terry takes off her top and licks her nipples, giving each side a fair amount of attention. He moves on to her lips. She's not into faking romance. He's not either and she can sense his indifference, allowing his lethargic attempt to eat her thoughts and crush her spirit. Before their half-assed romp goes any further, she puts a hand on his bare chest and says, "Hey, I'm not—")

"—in the mood."

"Ouch," Abbie said, jotting down more notes.

"Yeaaaah, and the other two attempts were just as good. Do you want to hear about them? It'll make for a great laugh later when you're out with friends."

"No." The psychiatrist waved her pen in the air. "No, not necessary."

Angela filled her lungs through her nose, then exhaled. The slow exercise did nothing to calm her. Her nerves were in turmoil, actively running up and down her entire body. Her heart pounded. She knew the sessions would help in the long run but she hated that weekly hour. Divulging secrets exhausted her until she had no more emotion left, went home feeling like a husk of her former self. "What do I do, Doc?"

"Can you be honest with me?"

Angela narrowed her eyes. "Of course. That's why I'm here, isn't it?"

"Do you still love Terry? And I don't mean out of some false sense of obligation. I'm talking about real love. Deep down, in the depths of your soul, do you still *love* him?"

It was a question she'd asked herself countless times before, so many she thought her brain would be quick to supply an answer. But the truth didn't come out that easily. She froze, her words lost in the swirl of memories and times past, happy and sad, significant and mundane.

"Don't think about it too long," Abbie said sternly, directing her eyes to her subject. "Wait too long and your mind will make up lies for you. Gut instinct—are you still head-over-heels-crazy-in-love with your husband, Angela Shepard?"

Angela replied, "Yes, I love him." The words came out sounding automated, and she wondered if Abbie sniffed out her lies.

"That's the truth?"

"Yes."

"Every day?"

Her eyes darted in different directions. They lingered on the wall behind Abbie, specifically on the framed painting of a bouquet of roses, one that looked oddly familiar. She couldn't shake the feeling that they were the same roses Terry occasionally bought on his way home from work. The flowers he staged on the rustic wrought-iron table near the stairs. It seemed impossible but her brain went fuzzy with a sudden flash of deja vu. Even the table upon which the vase rested looked like hers, copper-glazed legs and all.

"Yes, every day," she said, as if she were a robot reciting a programmed response. "We have our struggles like any couple. Especially after..." Her eyelids fluttered. "...but we do the best we can and move on. And there's love. Even if there's no sex, at least there's love."

The psychiatrist seemed satisfied with her summation and flashed a brief, mandatory smile. "Look at the time," she said, checking her watch. "Hour's up."

Thank God, Angela thought, rising from the couch that seemingly wanted to cradle her. She swore she felt arms wrapping themselves around her abdomen and pulling her back down. As she followed Abbie toward the front door, she glanced back. No arms, only the soft indentation where she had spent the last sixty minutes. As she left the office, the couch pulled on her memory strings, making her think she'd seen the furniture before, not in her living room, but somewhere else.

Maybe in a dream.

Maybe in the Everywhere.

***

She walked in through the front door and smelled dinner baking in the oven. When she turned the corner and stepped into the dining room, she immediately spotted the table and its enriched appearance; the lacy tablecloth, the pricey, ornate silverware they had received from Terry's parents on their wedding day, and the two vases overflowing with an array of flowers sporting chromatic petals. Terry bent over the table and set down a salad bowl and a plate full of mixed vegetables. He glanced up at her as she stopped and clutched the center of her chest in surprise.

"Hey, babe," he said with a faint smile.

"Hi," she said, not even realizing she was grinning. During the drive home, she had found it hard to concentrate, feeling empty and lost in her own mind. All those terrible feelings, those purged emotions, suddenly meant nothing as she glimpsed her husband setting the table. His hair was slicked back, just the way she liked it, and he'd thrown on an apron with the words *F*CK THE COOK* printed across the chest.

With a hand over her mouth, she chortled. "You're actually wearing that thing?"

He looked down, reading the words with a teeth-baring smile. "Oh, so you like my apron?"

"Yeah, I do. Where'd you find it?"

"It was buried in the linen closet. Remember when you bought it?"

She rolled her eyes. "Your birthday. Six years ago. It was supposed to be a gag gift."

"Figured I'd put it to good use." The corners of his mouth stretched.

She considered this behavior odd, and couldn't stop the question from forming in her head, from exiting her mouth. "Terry, what is all this?"

"What?"

She shrugged and glanced around the table, examining every plate, every special detail. "This."

"What do you mean?"

"You know." She knew how the stress of everything had affected him lately. During filming, the slightest criticism had turned into a full-blown argument. For the first few weeks anyway. Terry had shut down for the latter half of the season. He had barely spoken to her, which had prompted Barry to nudge the couple in a dark new direction; one Angela wasn't exactly prepared to travel down. "This isn't… you."

"What do you mean this isn't me?"

She disliked Terry when he played stupid, but, whatever trick he had stored up his sleeve, it came from a good place. She decided not to push him away, promised she wouldn't let the conversation veer into those familiar angry places.

"I just… everything's been so weird lately. I don't remember the last time you cooked dinner."

For a second, he looked like he wanted to do more than just argue— he looked like he wanted to explode. His face went slack and pale, his shoulders slumping. He breathed heavily through his mouth. Just when she expected him to lash out with some venomous remark about how she didn't love him anymore or about how far their marriage had fallen, his face broke into a huge grin. "I know. I haven't been a great husband lately."

Angela sighed. "No, Terry. That's not what I meant."

"It's okay," he said, almost jovially. "I admit it. I acted like an ass on the *Switch*. I embarrassed you. You don't have to say it if you don't want to. But I was a bona fide dickhead to you, and I'm sorry."

She didn't argue.

"I can't explain it. It was like I was someone else. Every day we were filming I thought, 'This isn't me. This isn't who I am.'" He frowned. "I'm better than that. *We're* better than that."

Angela nodded. "The show ended weird for both of us."

"Do you think we made a mistake?"

She placed the strap of her purse on the back of the chair in front her and sat down. She propped her head on her hands, as if her swollen cranium were too heavy for only her shoulders to support. "I don't feel any better. About this house. About what happened."

"That's how I feel, too." Terry scratched the little hair he had left on his head. Angela always found bald men, or balding men, somewhat repulsive. Then again, when she had met Terry almost ten years ago, he had an entire head full of long dark strands. But times change. So do tastes and she no longer minded the inevitable baldness. The thin wisps of hair and the visible dimpled texture of his scalp didn't exactly turn her on, but it wasn't as off-putting as she had expected. "I don't like what the show did to us."

"It was supposed to be a vacation."

They had spent two months in Vermont living in someone else's home, using someone else's amenities, sleeping in someone else's bed. *Living someone else's life.* The show was supposed to be an escape from reality but it hardly felt like one. They left with the intent of cleansing their souls but came back with another devil in their trunk. The cameras being shoved in their faces all-day-everyday issued a lot of stress, wedged a wrench between them, though they didn't help matters with their bickering and subsequent silent treatments. Barry, with his itinerary and list of demands, definitely complicated things. Their producer had been a hard-ass from day one. He acted like he was the director of a two-hundred-million-dollar Hollywood production. The guy had seemed chill and levelheaded during preproduction but the script flipped the second they stepped foot inside the Vermont house and started shooting.

Terry nodded. "Yeah. Now that I'm back here, though," he said, shivering, "feels like I never left."

"I know the feeling."

"What do we do?"

Angela shrugged. "I talked to the realtor earlier."

"Oh?"

"Yeah. No bites. Not so much as an inquiry. She wants to drop the price down another ten large."

"Well, that just sucks."

"I can't keep living here, Terry."

"I know, babe."

"This house. This town."

Terry sat down next to her and rubbed her shoulder. She leaned her head on his arm. "I grew up in Red River," he said. "It's the only place I've ever known."

"There are other towns," she told him, wrapping her arms around his midsection. "I can't live in this one anymore. It's tainted.

For the last eight months, a dark cloud's been floating over Red River and it hasn't left. The air tastes funny and always smells like smoke. I'm suffocating here."

He stroked her hair, pushing the golden clumps behind her ear. "We'll figure it out."

"Will we?"

"Of course." He kissed the top of her head. "We always do."

II.

THE THINGS THAT HAPPEN LATE AT NIGHT
ARE GONE IN THE MORNING

The clock on the nightstand read 3:03 a.m. when she kicked the covers off her body and got up to pee. She hustled to the bathroom, her bladder feeling like it was on the cusp of bursting. In fear of it emptying involuntarily, she elected to skip turning on the lights. Squatting on the toilet seat, she urinated in the dark. The sound of her piss hitting the water drowned out the drone of the air conditioning unit. As she relieved herself, she stared ahead at the bathtub, the site of many fond memories.

Ma-me.

Bubble baths.

Ma-me.

Bubble fights.

Ma-me.

A small ocean infested with rubber duckies and Power Rangers.

She forced herself to look away. Her eyes settled on the wall, immediately drawn to a peculiar white dot in the center of nearly-absolute darkness.

What the hell?

She wiped herself dry, yanked up her pajama bottoms, shut the toilet lid, flushed, and then crept across the bathroom to the far wall, her eyes glued to the small pinprick of light showing through.

Close enough, she knelt down before it.

Sure enough, she was face-to-face with a small hole in the wall, no bigger than a popcorn kernel, and it was letting in a considerable amount of light, heavenly white, the kind of brightness that would blind if shone directly into the pupil. Confused, Angela stood up and looked out the window, into the backyard. She peered down and saw nothing but shadows and the pale glow of the moon and the stars. Not enough light to produce the brightness she was seeing through the hole.

She shuddered when she glimpsed the overturned soil in the backyard. Terry had never bothered to put seed down after the police had combed it, leaving the whole area to look like a long row of prepped graves sans caskets. In some vague way, the backyard was indeed a burial site.

An empty one.

Angela bent down on one knee and stared at the small hole. She debated whether to look into it or not. Some feathery sensation swept across her neck, lacing her bones with chills. The hairs on her arms rose, becoming so erect her flesh hurt. She swallowed an invisible ball lodged in her throat. She didn't know why, but she felt she should wake Terry, that he should be here to witness this tiny phenomenon along with her. She looked over her shoulder, back toward the bedroom, contemplating whether to disturb her sleeping husband. Terry hated being roused for any reason, especially when something wasn't an emergency. He valued his sleep the same way bears did, dealing with intrusions just as angrily.

No, she wouldn't wake him. She turned back to the hole and closed one eye, putting the open one in front of the porthole.

(open water, choppy and endless, stretching beyond the fog-filled horizon. A small wooden ship she's seen in movies about pirates, complete with black sails and a crew of grimy bandits, twenty figures in all. They're distant. They're shouting. Barking commands at each other. She can't tell what they're saying, she's too far. They scurry around the deck, working, fighting, yelling. Suddenly, the water around the boat bubbles and churns. Something rises from below. Tentacles, eight total, larger than the ship in scale, ascend the misty-gray atmosphere, climbing the air well above the ship's mast. The men on the deck scatter in a panic. Some hurl themselves overboard, screaming. Others work

double-quick to carry out their captain's demands. Both acts prove futile as the tentacles come crashing down, smashing the ship to splinters. As the boat lay in ruin, Angela spots something else, just beyond the destruction: a lone figure, dark, shadowed, and watching. Not the scene. But her. The unknown shape spies her from a distance, floating above the flotsam with its arms folded across its chest, examining, waiting, ready for)

She pulled herself back, breathless. Her chest heaved and she placed her palm over her heart as if to stop it from leaping out of her chest. Another frosty, feathery something ran down her spine, the wintry sensation twisting and curling as it went. Her breath caught in her throat as she stepped away from the hole, the glimpse into her own private dreamworld.

What did I just see? She followed up her question with a more important one: *Was it real?*

She crossed the threshold and closed the bathroom door out of precaution. Surely whatever was behind the wall, the decimated pirate ship and the gargantuan sea beast, could not come through, but the situation disturbed her so much she couldn't help but think anything was possible.

She tiptoed across the carpet, over to her side of the bed, climbed in and pulled the covers up over her head. Sleep was far from her thoughts. Staring into the darkness for the next four hours, until Terry's alarm went off, Angela cried and questioned her own sanity.

———○———

On his knees, Terry craned his neck toward her. "You saw what now?"

"I told you. There was a tiny ship with little men on it."

Terry's eyes widened with alarm.

"Don't look at me like that."

He returned his eye to the hole. "I see pink insulation. It's an outside wall, love. Whatever created the hole didn't go through the sheathing."

"I know that *now*. I'm talking about what I saw last night."

"Uh-huh." Terry frowned. "And you saw… tentacles?"

Angela chewed on her lower lip and looked elsewhere. "Yes."

"I see. Uh, babe…"

"Don't."

"No, I believe you."

Angela eyed her husband warily. "You do?"

"Of course. I mean, I don't think you actually saw what you think you saw, but it's possible you had a waking nightmare of some sort."

"A waking nightmare?"

"Yeah, you know. Like you were awake but still dreaming. That's a thing…" He said this last part as if trying to convince himself it was true. "Look, I'm no doctor. But I think the stress of coming back here has put your mind in a frenzy. Hell, last night, I had some strange dreams myself."

"Oh really?"

"Yep."

"What were they of?"

Terry arched his brow and looked up as if the images in his brain were projected on the ceiling. "I don't remember exactly. But I do remember them being strange." He sighed and reached out to grab her hand. She let him. He squeezed gently and, for the moment, she felt safe and secure, the fear for her own sanity had all but subsided. "We'll get through this. We will. We just need a little more time. Once the checks from the show start rolling in, we'll start getting serious about this house hunting thing. We can move anywhere you like."

Her eyes expanded. "You mean that?"

"Yes, I do."

"What happened to 'Red River is the only place I know' mumbo-jumbo?"

Terry shook his head adamantly. "Don't worry about that. I was being selfish. I want you to be happy. We can move anywhere you want. I'll even go to Pennsylvania so we can be near your folks, if that's what you want."

She considered this with a smile. "Well, not too close."

"I love you, Angela Shepard."

"I love you, too, Terry Shepard."

He got to his feet and kissed her on the lips, the sensual touch lasting for a long time, much longer than she expected.

III.

SEASON PREMIERE

They gathered on the couch with a bucket of popcorn and two glass bottles of Coca-Cola. The season premiere of *Let's Switch Houses!* was a commercial or two away from starting. Barry had called them an hour earlier, asking if they were excited or nervous and how they planned to celebrate once the show had aired. He had returned to being the Barry he'd been before they had started filming, amiable and kind, not the monster he had become on set. She told him "pretty excited", though that wasn't the truth, or close to it. *Nervous* didn't even cover it. No, Angela *feared* seeing herself on the small screen. No one would consider her overweight, but the old adage "the cameras add ten pounds" crept up on her like a ninja ten minutes before show time and she immediately started checking her stomach for evidence of chub rolls, the backs of her arms for hanging flab. She found none, but the old expression continued to repeat itself inside her head regardless. Not only was she scared of looking plump, but she also wondered how Barry and the post-production team would depict her. She had given them all aspects of her role as Terry's other half—the somber wife who tried to keep her husband happy, the sad wife who held onto past mistakes, and the angry wife who sometimes took her frustrations out on her husband—they were all there, all caught on film for the world to see. It was up to the editors which one they wanted to portray, which "Angela" they thought prospective audiences would relate to best.

She suddenly had a very bad feeling about this.

"You okay?" Terry asked, shoveling a fistful of popcorn in his mouth.

"Yeah, just a little nervous."

"We're about to be stars."

"That's what I'm kinda nervous about." She lied. She didn't think the show would launch her into celebrity stardom like other reality television stars. She wasn't aspiring to be a real housewife or a castaway survivor or reach *The Bachelorette* status. She was going to be Angela, the woman who'd taken her slice of the American Dream and ruined it with one simple mistake, one *terrible* moment.

They're not going to pity you, she thought. *They're going to hate you.*

She had already achieved local celebrity status because of what had happened, in fact, "the tragedy" had trended on Facebook for almost twenty-four hours when the news initially broke. So in a way, the public already knew her. *About* her. And, from what she'd been told, pitied her. Was rooting for her to come out of this on top. Maybe that was why Barry and the other producers had selected her. Because she needed this. She needed a victory.

No, she thought. *I deserve one.*

(Ma-me)

Or maybe they had chosen her because they had seen dollar signs when they closed their eyes and pictured her face. No one really knew what happened that day, no one but Angela

(Ma-me)

so maybe Barry thought having her on the show would reveal some important clue, something the police had missed, something the lead detectives had never pieced together. Maybe the whole purpose of the show was to *catch* her.

But there was nothing to catch. She knew that. She also knew they needed the money so they could afford to get out of this godforsaken place and never look back. The salary from the show wouldn't provide that kind of freedom on its own but it was a good start.

"And now for our feature presentation," said the off-screen host.

Terry nudged his wife. "Here we go, babe." He watched the flatscreen with childlike enthusiasm, something Angela couldn't even pretend to match.

The show opened with, *"Hi, I'm Angela."*

"And I'm Terry."

In unison: *"And we live here!"*

[Angela and Terry point to their house in the background]

"Oh, God," Angela said, covering her eyes. "This is so corny."

"Relax," Terry told her, rubbing her knee affectionately. "You won't enjoy it if you're criticizing the whole time."

"How can I not?" She almost found her smile. Almost.

[Cuts to a woman, mid-sixties. "I'm Rosalyn Jeffries and I live here." The woman speaks with little emotion, like the words are being forcefully drawn from her by outside influences. Her accent suggests she's European, from where we can't quite put our finger on. She points at the house where Angela and Terry had spent the last two months, a small ranch on a block all by itself, back facing a lush Vermont forest. It's mid-April and there are leftover patches of snow on the ground.

The scene quick-cuts to the house's interior. We see the woman sitting on her couch. Like us, this is the first time Angela has seen her. She has short curly hair. Earrings dangle from low-hanging lobes, the jewelry reaching her shoulders. She's wearing a black and turquoise shawl, making her appear like one of those phony palm readers offering five-dollar sessions at the local flea market. "I lost my husband six months ago, and…" she goes on and tells us how Carl was her best friend, her soulmate, and how empty life has become since his passing.]

"Hm," Terry said. "She seems… nice."

Angela rolled her eyes. "She looks… I dunno. Kinda crazy?"

"Is it the cape she's wearing?"

Angela burst out laughing. "I believe it's called a shawl."

"Never heard of it."

"Oh, come on."

"Honestly."

"You're so stupid sometimes."

"Yeah, but you love me."

They embraced. At the moment, things felt good. Things felt right. For the first time in a long time, Angela believed their marriage was slowly mending, fixing itself naturally. *It's like he forgot. It's like he doesn't blame me anymore.* Didn't her psychiatrist predict that? She distinctly remembered Abbie explaining the grieving process in great detail and how natural it was for Terry to blame her, how his cancerous feelings would abate with time. *God, she was right.* She gripped her husband as if she were sliding off the edge of the world, and squeezed.

They continued watching.

[Inside the Vermont house, Angela and Terry are unpacking. The room is

painted Caribbean blue. There is a dreamcatcher hanging over the bed's bear-brown comforter. We cut to the confessional booth where Angela is telling us about the tragedy. "And then... {we do not speak his name} was gone. Just like that." She excuses herself while her eyes begin to water and leak. We cut to Terry in the booth and he stares at us with a somber expression, his lower lip quivering. He swallows and his Adam's apple jumps in his throat. "We don't like to talk about it," he tells us. "Sometimes it's best if we think it never happened. But it's hard." He pauses and the instrumental music drops out. Barry says: "Do you blame your wife for what happened?" Terry hesitates, but, in the end, he shakes his head and says, "No. God, no. She would never do anything to hurt {we do not speak his name}.]

"Is that true?" Angela asked, peering up at him.

"Of course, baby." Terry kissed the crown of her head. "I never blamed you."

"Even right after it happened?"

Terry paused, longer than he had on screen when Barry had asked him a similar question. "Things were so crazy. I can't remember everything I felt. I remember feeling so... so goddamn numb all the time. During the entire investigation, I felt..."

"Empty?"

Terry nodded. "Yeah. Yeah, that's probably the best way to describe it. Like I was still in control of myself but also like I was watching myself through someone else's eyes. Like my life was a movie and I was the only audience member."

"Yeah, I felt that way, too."

"In retrospect, I wish we had talked more during those days."

"Yeah, me too."

[Rosalyn Jeffries is sitting on their couch, where the Shepards sit now, watching her daily programs. We cut to her in the booth: "There is an emptiness in my heart since Carl passed. I spend a lot of time watching television, reading books, catching up on current events. Carl was my life, you see. We did everything together. And I do mean everything. Since we retired, not a minute had gone by that we weren't at each other's sides. We had no children, so... it was always that way."

Off-screen, Barry asks: "Do you still talk to your husband, Rosalyn?"

She looks off camera as if Barry had just asked her to solve a quantum physics equation. She scoffs. "Of course. He visits me every single day."]

"Creepy," Terry said, wincing from the chill erecting the hair on his arms.

Angela shook off a serpentine shiver from her spine. "Super creepy."

The show went on for another twenty minutes. It followed the standard season opener formula where the characters were introduced, shown engaging in mundane activities and daily chores, while intermittently speaking about why they were there, what their lives were about, and how they felt the switch could help them.

During Angela and Terry's segment, they had traveled down the Vermont mountainside and into town where they had ended up at a small village of privately-owned shops. The shots brought back some pleasant memories and in that moment Angela smelled the sweet citrusy fragrance of fruit-scented candles. The scene cut back to Rosalyn driving down Route 9, into the heart of Red River. The roads had been congested as usual; it was a Friday night on the Jersey Shore and the traffic flowed with unpleasant southbound visitors. She had pulled into the Red River Mall parking lot, climbed out of her black Oldsmobile, and headed inside.

That was when the television began to flicker with intermittent static and—

[We're back in the house. Rosalyn Jeffries is kneeling on the living room floor, praying in front of the television displaying only static. Her eyes are closed, her lips are moving, and her naked body is still. We're looking at her from behind and only see the weathered, wrinkly skin of the old woman, her backside, her—"]

"What the hell?" Angela asked, launching herself from her husband's side, nearly jumping off the couch.

[Rosalyn begins to chant. The words are indecipherable, but they sound ancient, fragments of a language that predated man. A language one might associate with some kind of ritual, maybe satanic, since that's always the most popular association. On screen, static ripples down the picture, a minor interference. A low tone, like tinnitus, can be heard in the background, accompanying the woman's ritualistic vocalization.]

"Terry, I don't like this."

"What is it, babe?"

[The woman rises up, tossing her hands in the air and throwing her head back. She's shouting the words now, stamping her feet in some tribal dance. At the television, she begins to bark like a dog. Next, she folds her arms into wings and flaps them up and down, clucking like a chicken and jerking her head forward and backward in spastic fashion. The camera fades out so we can see more of the room and less of the naked woman and the television with no picture. The new shot reveals the walls and their new décor; ceremonial symbols have been engraved in all four, large shapes incorporating circles and triangles, hexagons and octagons, trapezoids

and ellipses. They glow in the darkness like molten lava. They pulse along with the woman's dance, burning bright with her movements and fluid gyrations, fading during those brief seconds of inactivity. We watch as the woman bends down, picks up a limp object, and holds it in front of the television. It's a dead chicken. The woman takes the knife she also had staged on the floor, brings the metal to the chicken's neck, digs the blade in, and begins to saw...]

"What the fuck, Terry?" Angela shouted, her voice cracking.

Terry jumped onto the couch as if the carpet beneath his feet had suddenly become hot coals. He checked his wife to see if she was okay, feeling her forehead for a fever. He corralled her close with both arms and, during his heroic reaction, he knocked over the bowl, spilling popcorn across the couch and onto the floor. "What is it, babe? What's wrong?"

"What do you mean what's wrong?" she screamed so loud her vocal cords burned. Eyes locking onto the disturbed picture, she pointed at the insanity unfolding before her. "Don't you see what she's doing? Don't you see what she did in our house?"

Terry opened his mouth to speak, but

[Blood rains from the chicken's opened neck, torrents of black syrupy liquid splashing the carpet. The woman looks back at us, craning her neck slowly as if she isn't sure what's behind her, unsure if she should look back and confront the possibility of some unspeakable terror, some unnamed thing that has taken the house under its spell, its power, flashing its unlimited control...]

"God, what did she do in our house?" Angela cried, tears spilling over the rims of her eyes.

"Angela, I have no idea what you're talking about," he replied, rubbing her back. They were on the floor. Angela knelt on all fours, glancing up at the television. Terry bent on one knee beside her, comforting her with his left hand, parading his fingers down her spine. "Calm down, you're freaking me out."

"Freaking you out?" she squawked. *"A goddamn ritual sacrifice took place in our home and you want me to calm the fuck down?"*

Terry's hand stopped halfway up her back. She stared into his eyes and saw something there that induced more shivers than the unfolding events captured on camera; her husband was absolutely clueless. He hadn't seen what she saw.

"Angela," he said, surprisingly serene. Sweat dripped off the end of his nose. "What in God's name are you talking about?"

[The woman turns and faces the camera. Her eyes are whited out like small marble orbs. A messy tangle of hair, thick as yarn, hides most of her facial features. Her lumpy breasts droop like half-empty sacks of laundry. Her stomach folds in three rolls, the bottom covering the top of her pubic hair. Moles the size of quarters pepper her doughy, dimpled flesh. With pure white eyes, she stares at the camera, at us, the audience, and in a harsh, long-time-smoker voice she says, "Stay out of this house."]

Angela couldn't breathe as the words left the woman's mouth; feeling like an invisible claw reached down her throat and punctured her lungs. Nothing involving her body seemed to work except her bladder. The warmth of fresh urine spilled down her leg, tickling her flesh.

"Oh, Jesus," Terry said, immediately smelling the bodily waste. Panic infiltrated his voice. "Oh, honey. What the... what the hell is happening to you?"

"She..."

"She what? What did you see?"

["Stay out of this house," the woman says again. Then, in a voice no one would consider feminine, nor masculine, but a strange amalgamation of both, she repeats, "Stay out of this house." The throaty voice keeps changing, growing deeper, but the message remains the same: "Stay out of this house. Stay out of this house. STAY OUT OF THIS HOUSE."]

"She..."

"Angela, talk to me." He held his wife closely.

"What she did in our house..."

"She didn't do anything in our house," Terry said, shaking her, trying to snap her back to reality. "Angie, she didn't do anything."

["Stay out of this house."]

Terry leaned into her ear. "She's getting an ice cream cone from the food court."

[Stay out, Ma-me.]

Ma-me.

Angela opened her eyes and saw Rosalyn Jeffries accepting a cone from a young teenager manning the ice cream stand in the center of the mall. The old woman immediately started licking the frosty treat, catching the runny cream with her tongue before it reached her fingers.

"What?" Angela huffed, breathless.

"That's it," Terry said. "Calm down, honey. Everything's all okay." He rocked her back and forth, cradling her in his arms.

"What happened? She was… and now she's…"

"I don't know but it's okay now. You're okay."

"You didn't see it?"

"See what?"

Ma-Me.

"The woman. In our living room. Dancing?"

Terry looked down at her, his usual complexion escaping his face. "No, babe. I didn't see anything. Are you okay? Are you feeling all right? I mean, Jesus, Angela, you pissed yourself."

She'd forgotten about that. She looked down and saw her pajamas and the dark wet stain running from her crotch to her ankle. The sour smell permeated the air, biting her senses.

"Why don't we get you off the floor?"

Her husband helped her to her feet.

"I'm so embarrassed."

"Don't be."

She threw her arms around him and roped him in. In his ear, she whispered, "What the hell is happening to me?"

If Terry wondered the same thing, he didn't say. "You're okay. You're fine. Let's get you showered and we'll talk about this tomorrow."

She followed him past the table featuring the vase of flowers and headed upstairs. She looked back into the living room the moment before the 60-inch screen disappeared behind the hallway ceiling; she swore the picture obscured, warped in a frenzy of black and white pixels, and then she listened as the soft crunch of static buzzed between her ears.

IV.

THEY MAKE PILLS FOR THAT

I'm going to change up your prescription," Abbie said, scribbling on her notepad.

Angela sighed. "You think I'm nuts, don't you?"

Without looking up, Abbie shook her head. "No, dear. I don't. Sometimes stress gets to be too much and begins to manifest physically. Common problem amongst my patients."

"So... I'm hallucinating?"

Abbie paused for a beat, and then glanced up. "Well, you don't believe sea monsters exist inside of your bathroom wall, do you?"

"No... but..."

"No one else in America saw the old woman cut off a chicken's head but you."

"Yeah, but it seemed so real."

"Honey, I was one of *Switch's* fifteen million viewers and I can guarantee you they didn't air a ritual sacrifice on cable television."

Angela wanted to laugh or maybe cry; she wasn't sure which. She kept replaying the nightmarish scenario over and over again; hoping the more she relived the horrible fantasy, the less it'd feel like reality. Didn't work, though, in fact, the more she revisited last night, the more her brain revolted and the more her skull felt like it might split in half.

"I'm losing my mind," she admitted.

"Well, it hasn't been easy. What happened to you and Terry was awful, something no two parents should ever have to experience. You'll never fully recover, but, over time, things will get better. Manageable." She paused, placing the end of her pen on her lips. "You'll deal."

"Terry's been nice to me lately. We haven't fought for a whole week."

"I'm glad to hear."

Tears eminent, Angela sniffled. "I think he loves me again."

"Of course he does. He never stopped."

Angela fought back the sadness, the burning sensation seeping into her eyes.

Abbie leaned forward and gently placed a hand on Angela's knee. "I want you to take these pills. They'll help curb the hallucinations. But your usual pharmacy won't carry it. It's a… let's call it an experimental drug."

Angela looked at the script. "Is it safe?"

"Of course. It's just not FDA approved. Yet. You can purchase it at Robinson's over in Carver's Grove, only about twenty minutes from here. In fact, I'll call it in. It'll be ready by the time you get there."

"And it stops hallucinations?"

"Yes. And, if for whatever reason it doesn't, call me immediately and we'll get you on something else. However, I'm confident this will work. It's worked on my other patients who have experienced similar symptoms."

Angela took the script, folded it, and buried it inside her purse. "Thanks, Doc."

"My pleasure."

○——————◇——————○

The drive to Robinson's in Carver's Grove took exactly twenty minutes. She listened to the classic rock station the entire way over, and they were playing Bon Jovi's *Slippery When Wet* in its entirety, an album she had listened to countless times when she was about twelve. The music brought back some great memories of her rocking out in her bedroom, belting out the lyrics at the top of her lungs while jumping on her bed and strumming her air guitar, annoying her parents and siblings to no end.

She parked outside of Robinson's, stepped out the car, and headed inside. Robinson's wasn't your ordinary pharmacy. Perusing the aisles, she found not a single brand name stocked on the shelves.

Every remedy had been made with "natural" ingredients. A lot of the packaging looked thrown together by some amateur graphic designer who had just started to experiment with Photoshop.

She passed the book and magazine rack, noticing they stocked the same bestsellers as every other local pharmacy. She stopped and picked up the new Kim Harrison book, flipped through its pages, then set it back on the shelf figuring she could stop at the local library on the way home. She bypassed the row of colorful magazine covers and headed straight for the rear of the store, where the young lady behind the counter was bagging a few prescriptions for the only customer in line, a tall man with a fedora and circular-rimmed spectacles. After she finished, she wished the man a good day and asked Angela if there was anything she needed help with.

"Yes, actually," Angela said timidly, approaching the counter. "Dr. Wilson called in a prescription for me?"

"Ah, yes." Angela examined the girl's name tag, which read, "Kandi." Kandi turned to a small box teeming with prescriptions and began rifling through. "Shepard, right?"

"That's right."

"Very cool," she said, and then read off the label to Angela. The name of the drug sounded like the technical name for a species of previously undiscovered sea creatures.

Angela shrugged. "I guess that's right."

"Here you go," Kandi said, handing over the bag.

"How much do I owe?"

The girl shook her head. "Nothing."

"Nothing?"

"All paid for."

"What do you mean?"

The girl rolled her eyes. "I mean, it's already been taken care of. You owe nothing."

"How… who?"

Kandi shrugged, her lips parting into an amiable smile. "I don't know. Doesn't say. But it's in our system. Maybe Dr. Wilson?"

"Why would she?"

Kandi sighed and lifted her shoulders. "I don't know, Mrs. Shepard. There are some good people out there in the world. What can I tell you? Never look a gift horse in the mouth and all that."

"Well," she said, hesitant to take the bag from her. "Thanks."

"I watched the show, by the way."

"Oh?" Angela forced herself to smile. No one had recognized her in public yet and that first sip of celebrity tasted strange. "Thank you."

"Yeah…" she said, her mouth pulling taut, the skin around her eyes forming deep wrinkles. "I'm so sorry for your loss and everything you and your husband went through. My heart bleeds for you both."

Angela tried to keep the smile intact, but she felt it slip. "That's… that's very kind of you to say."

Kandi nodded, changing her demeanor back to its original salesperson facade. "He's still alive, you know," she bubbled.

Angela went rigid as her blood froze in her veins. Her skin hardened with gooseflesh and her heart rattled around her chest. She felt her eyes expand, nearly pop out of their sockets. Words died in the desert her mouth had become. She managed to squeak out, "What did you say?", but she hardly sounded like herself.

A smile broke across Kandi's face. "In here," she said, pointing to the center of her chest. "In your hearts."

The girl's choice of words wasn't easy to shake. Angela forced herself to smile back, but she didn't need a mirror to tell she was grimacing with uneasiness. She closed her eyes and nodded as if to say, *okay-you-scared-me-shitless-but-now-I-understand.* "I see…"

"I'm sorry," Kandi said, losing the smile. "I didn't mean to overstep my boundaries."

"No, it's fine. It's just… my husband and I don't discuss it much. It's strange hearing other people talk about it."

"Yeah, I sorta gathered that from the show."

Something tugged at Angela's throat. "Yes. Well…"

"Have a great day, Mrs. Shepard. I look forward to experiencing more of your journey."

She waved the girl goodbye, but before she turned and headed for the exit, she noticed Kandi kneading the crucifix dangling from her neck and whispering quietly.

She swore the girl was praying.

Or reciting some ancient verse.

Whatever it was, it wasn't English.

The second she stepped outside, Angela opened the small bottle and tapped a pill into her palm. She popped it in her mouth, cocked her head back, and swallowed it dry. She pressed a hand to her head to feel if she was warm, if maybe she was coming down with a fever. She was achy and exhausted, but her forehead felt cool, normal. She took a deep breath and wondered if she was going plain crazy.

Maybe that's it. I'm past the breaking point my mother always warned us about. Or maybe I'm just a fucking whacko.

Angela crossed the parking lot and headed for her car. Her eyes were immediately drawn across the lot, focusing on a familiar vehicle.

[The woman pulls her Oldsmobile into the Red River Mall parking lot, gets out, and heads to the food court where she buys a two-scoop ice cream sundae.]

The woman. She was slumped in the driver's seat, her eyes scanning the downtown landscape. Watching. Waiting. Spying.

Oh God.

As their eyes met and locked onto each other, Angela felt the bottom of her stomach plummet. Her bladder filled and she did everything within her power to keep from wetting herself. She dropped her small shopping bag on the pavement and began walking toward the woman's vehicle, entranced by her sudden presence. *Come to me,* she almost heard the woman whisper in her ear. In the distance, the Oldsmobile cranked to life. Angela quickened her pace. *Come to me.* The smell of gasoline was heavy in the air. She almost choked on it.

Come to me.

Angela broke out into a run, speeding—

Come to me.

HONK! HONK!

A blue sedan knocked into her, launching her a few inches off the ground. Angela immediately sprang to her feet, looking back at the young driver who had tapped her.

"What's the hell's wrong with you, lady?" the kid asked, irritated as if he were the one sprawled on the concrete.

Angela put her palms up to signify she was okay. "I'm sorry, I'm sorry. I just…" She looked over to where Rosalyn Jeffries had been parked.

The old woman was gone.

"Shit," Angela said, pinching the bridge of her nose. "Shit, shit, shit."

"Are you okay, lady?" the kid asked with the same amount of frustration. "Do I need to call an ambulance?"

"No, I'm fine." She scanned the streets for evidence of the Oldsmobile, but the woman had disappeared behind a steady flow of mid-morning traffic.

"Well, watch where you're going next time," the kid said as he cruised by her.

"Thanks for the advice," she replied, under her breath, while heading back for the dropped prescription.

The entire way home she couldn't shake that *I'm-being-followed* feeling.

V.

LOVE WILL SEE US THROUGH TO THE BITTER END

Dinner was quiet. Too quiet. Terry had prepared another one of his stellar home-cooked meals, and Angela spent most of the time peering down at her food, nudging the lemon-garnished chicken and buttered broccoli around her plate.

"Not hungry?" Terry asked.

Angela set down her fork. "Not really."

"What have you eaten today?"

She rubbed her forehead, trying to remember. "I had a peanut butter and jelly sandwich earlier."

"That's it?"

Shutting her eyes, she breathed deeply through her nose. "Haven't had much of an appetite lately."

"Since the…"

She nodded.

"Maybe you should see someone."

She gulped. *Does he already know?* How could he? She had been so careful. The bills were sent electronically to an e-mail address she had secretly created behind her husband's back. She felt bad doing so, but it was necessary. Abbie had promised to keep their sessions private—patient confidentiality and all that—and Angela knew that was a promise she wouldn't break, despite her repeated recommendations for couple's therapy.

"I already have," she said, the words slipping out before she could fully think them through.

"Really?" He sounded genuinely surprised.

"Yes. For a while now. I'm sorry I didn't tell you. I thought you'd be angry."

He set down his fork, resting the utensil on the edge of his plate. "Why would I be angry?"

She averted her eyes from her trembling fingers and stared at him. "I don't know. Thought maybe you'd see it as a sign of weakness. Like I couldn't cope with what's happening. That you'd think I'm crazy and not love me anymore."

"Honey…" He pushed himself away from the table and stood up. He meandered around the table and hugged his wife. "Baby, I would never think that of you."

She sobbed into his chest, soaking his shirt with tears. "You were so distant after those first few months."

"I know, babe. I know. It was my fault. I was… I didn't know how to cope with it, either." He planted a kiss on her forehead and let his lips linger. "Tell me about this psychiatrist."

Pulling away from him, she collected herself. She dabbed idling tears with a napkin. "Her name is Abigail Wilson. She's very nice. Today she gave me a prescription to help with the… the… hallucinations."

"That's great, honey."

"Promise you're not mad?"

"No, I'm actually proud you're getting help."

She laughed incredulously. "Proud? Okay, who are you and what did you do with my husband?"

Terry clicked his tongue against the roof of his mouth. That patented smirk-frown rested crookedly on his face. "Babe, I'm here to support you. Whatever you are going through, we're in this together. I'm here to the bitter end."

"Love will see us through?"

"Always."

Angela smiled. "You know, Abbie wanted to bring you in for a couple's session."

Terry grinned. "Well, I don't know about that. That's kinda where I draw the line."

"I told her you'd say something like that."

They shared a chuckle. Then Terry dropped his smirk and frown act, and his face went rigid. "No, but in all seriousness, if you think it'd help…"

"That means a lot to me."

He kissed her again. "Come. Follow me." He grabbed her hand.

"Where are we going?"

"I have something to show you."

In the candlelit room, they undressed each other. Terry kissed her neck gently and squeezed her breasts. She closed her eyes and grabbed him. He lifted her into his arms as she jumped up and wrapped her legs around him. He laid her down on the bed with more force than she had anticipated.

She opened her eyes. He stared down at her. She closed her eyes again and her body was instantly injected with a pleasure she'd long since forgotten.

"Terry," she breathed into his ear as he started to maneuver around inside her, knocking his hips against her bottom. As their bodies rocked in perfect harmony, she bit her lip, so hard her tongue detected metallic flavors.

Love will get us through…

"I love you," she whispered in a hot breath. "I love you so much."

…to the bitter end.

She cried.

When it was over, she cried some more.

VI.

IF NOT HERE, WHERE ARE WE?

She awoke to an empty bed. Terry had already left for work, gone hours before. In place of his body was a plate of chocolate-chip waffles topped with a puddle of strawberry syrup and a heap of whipped cream, a folded note tucked neatly beneath it. She snatched the note first and unfolded the paper as if it contained the code to disarm a nuclear warhead. With giggly schoolgirl joy, she read her husband's message:

Babe,

Last night was pure magic. I love you. I feel whole again.

Terry

I feel whole again.

Those words stuck. She felt something too, and though the past had broken her, battered her once high spirits, that morning she awoke reconnected with some semblance of her former self. The world seemed brighter, sharper. Her vision crisper. Senses fired on all cylinders, her energy restored. Angela opened the bedroom window and let in a breeze carrying earthly fragrances, oddly euphoric, scents that traveled up her nasal cavities, into her brain, coating her mind and soul with a comforting shiver, a message from the world saying everything would be okay and it'd all work out in the end. That the journey ahead would be long and hard, and sometimes uncomfortable and often grueling, but in the end, she'd survive and become almost whole again.

The moment lasted about thirty seconds, the time it took for her to notice the black Oldsmobile parked across the street. Her stomach lurched, the taste of sickness entering the back of her throat. The tantalizing aroma quickly faded as her nerves swam fiercely, throwing her body into a state of perpetual chaos. Panic stabbed her chest, causing her heart to pump like a locomotive piston. The attack was so strong her arms and legs tingled with numbness, and, for a second, she thought someone had cut open her veins. She checked herself to make sure her flesh was free from injury, and of course, she found her skin unmarked. Her eyes returned to the Oldsmobile and searched for the driver.

The front seat was empty. So was the back. There was no one on the sidewalk. No one at all.

Where is she?

She poked her head out the window and glanced around the property, down the street; the woman was nowhere in her line of sight. Her mind kicked into a frenzy of terrible thoughts, recalling the obscene images from the other night.

Oh God, she thought, *does the woman still have the key?*

She couldn't remember giving Barry back the keys to the Vermont house, but realized she wouldn't have because Terry handled those details. But still…

What if she still has the key?

Angela wondered if the woman had been in the house between the hours Terry left for work and the end of her long nap. She pictured the old witch standing over her while she slept, chanting and dancing, conjuring the spirits of another realm of existence (*the Everywhere*), a place where demons slept and waited, biding their time to cross over worlds. She imagined the woman dangling a chicken over her naked flesh, digging a blade beneath the bird's skin, the savage removal of its head and the freshets of blood raining down on her. She envisioned the woman's words having the power to open the walls and give birth to an ancient gateway, granting access to a fiery underworld harboring horned beasts and otherworldly creatures eagerly awaiting the flesh of God's precious, chosen creations.

Her cell rang, pulling her out of the twisted reveries.

She dashed across the room, over to the nightstand and grabbed her phone.

"Terry!" she answered, breathless and sounding manic.

"Morning, love. Did you enjoy my surprise?" She knew he was grinning by the tone of his voice. "I wish I could have cuddled you all morning, but, you know, duty calls."

"Terry, I need help."

A slight pause. "What's the matter?"

"She's here."

"Who's there?"

"The woman."

"What woman?"

"From the show, Terry. From the *goddamn* show."

"Rosalyn Jeffries?"

"Yes!"

Another pause. "Well, is she nice?"

"Terry!"

"What?"

"I think… she… I think she's here to *kill me.*"

Terry bellowed with laughter. "Baby, please. That's ridiculous. Why on God's-Green-Earth would she want to kill you?"

"Because…"

"Baby, you can't be serious." Another beat. Then: "Wait. Are you serious?"

"I don't know. Maybe. I have a bad feeling. Whatever's been going on with me lately, I think it's…"

Terry waited. "Yes?"

"I think it's her fault. It's like she's done something to the house. Put a curse on us or something."

"Put a curse on us? Do you know how crazy that sounds?"

She did, which was part of the problem. She hardly believed it herself but she couldn't shake the feeling her intuition was correct, that the woman had jinxed the house and was now haunting her from afar.

"Yes, Terry. I absolutely know how fucking crazy that sounds. But I can't… I can't explain what's happening to me any other way." She gulped. "She infected this place."

"What do you want me to do?" She could envision her husband pinching the bridge of his nose and shutting his eyes, his patented move when his patience was worn.

"I don't know."

"I can call the police. But they'll be pissed if the woman came by to drop off a cake and a jar of cookies."

The doorbell chimed.

"Shit, Terry. She's at the door."

"Okay, so what am I doing?"

"Call them. Call the police."

"Fine."

They hung up.

Angela, crouching, stalked out of the bedroom, down the hall, and stopped when she reached the top of the stairs. She stayed there, spying the front door, eyeing the shadow stationed behind the decorative full lite of obscured glass.

God, what does she want from me?

"Mrs. Shepard?" the woman called. Her voice matched the accent used on the show, and hearing the inflection live and in person sent a chill streaking down Angela's spine. "Mrs. Shepard, I know you're home. I understand we don't know each other, but I feel we need to talk."

Remaining silent, Angela sat down on the top step, clenched her eyes shut, and listened. She thought about replying, having an actual conversation with the woman, intending to keep her there long enough until the police arrived, but, in the end, she decided she didn't want any communication with her. Not with the woman who'd hexed her home.

That witch.

"I know my time is limited," the woman said. "You've probably already phoned the police, but, if you think you need help, please seek me out. I think you understand my meaning." The woman paused, giving Angela one last opportunity to respond. "Good day, Mrs. Shepard."

With that, the shadow abated. She heard footsteps as the woman walked down the stoop. Outside noise became distant as she shuffled across the yard, opened her car door, closed it, started the Oldsmobile, and drove off.

I think you understand my meaning, the old woman had said, and those words calloused Angela's arms and legs in gooseflesh.

Ten minutes later, the police arrived. Two officers, younger than she, took her statement. She told them where the woman lived and about the show. They said they were familiar with *Switch!*; their wives were big fans of previous seasons and they had watched this season's premiere. They told her they'd be real heroes if they Snapchatted a picture to their significant others. She reluctantly obliged, hoping the gracious act would motivate them to take her matter more seriously than they had initially appeared to.

When asked, "Why do you feel threatened, Mrs. Shepard?" Angela simply shrugged and said, "I don't know. That's just how I feel."

She neglected to mention how she felt hexed.

Night fell on Trenton Road and shadows sauntered across the Shepard's bedroom. There was no sex that night. Terry was exhausted from cranking a wrench all day and fell asleep about ten seconds after his cheek landed on the pillow. Angela stirred awake, thinking, revisiting the woman's words, everything she had said. *We need to talk.* What did she want to talk about? The curse she laid upon their house? God, as if she wasn't dealing with enough problems, now Angela had to deal with a witch and her unjustified vendetta against her and her husband. *We need to talk.*

In your dreams, she thought, and then wondered if dreams were safe from witches and dark magic. Could dreams be a place of refuge? A safe haven? A reprieve from evil? Angela didn't think so. Thinking back to her "hallucinations", which were much like dreams, she thought the witch could get to her from any state of mind—asleep, awake, sober, or intoxicated. The woman's *touch* knew no boundaries.

Angela threw off her covers and headed downstairs for a glass of water. For the next half hour, she drank fluids and stared out the back window, across the muddy expanse that made up the backyard. She wondered when Terry would level the dirt and plant seed. She was tired of seeing their once Irish-green lawn dead and impoverished. Even though she hadn't stepped foot out there since *[we do not speak his name]* was alive, the plot was still an eyesore and, in all likelihood, degraded the selling value of the property. Maybe that was what held them back. Not the tragedy, but the unruly condition of the sizable backyard. She thought she'd make the chore a priority this weekend, to motivate Terry and get it done. If they could afford to pay someone, she would have taken care of it the second the cops were finished rooting around back there, concluding their lengthy investigation. She was sure Terry would start it now, especially if she asked in a certain, flirty way; after all, he *was* in love with her again.

Angela made her way past the table with the flowers, up the stairs, and toward the bedroom. From the end of the hall, she spotted a blue light glowing underneath the door. She hadn't remembered falling asleep with the television on. It was rare Terry awoke in the middle of the night—he slept like a drunken bear, as well as often waking like one—and she couldn't recall a time in their twelve years of marriage when he had woken up and turned on the tube.

Strange, she thought; although, considering what she'd witnessed over the past week, a television turning itself on could hardly be considered peculiar.

She approached the bedroom door and gripped the brass knob. Her hand immediately bounced off the hardware as if some magical spell were placed to repel her touch. All at once, a rush of pain filled her palm, and she looked down to see several layers of her skin had melted away like excessively microwaved cheese. The burning sensation crawled throughout her entire hand and climbed up her arm. Shaking her palm wildly, she screamed out as the white-hot pain cranked up the intensity.

"Fuck! Goddammit, fuck!"

She blew on her disfigured palm, but the wind did little to temper the burn.

"Terry?" she shouted at the door.

The house responded, pushing open the bedroom door. She recoiled, shrinking back into the shadows of the hall. Blue light escaped the room and spilled across the carpet. Quick pulses of white flickered from inside the bedroom like lightning streaking behind clusters of midnight-gray clouds. An awful burning stench carried its way from the room to her nose. The malodor was enough to trigger her gag reflex. She almost lost her dinner on her way back to the door.

"Terry…" she said, approaching the bedroom slowly, as if the floorboards might give out beneath her. "Terry, talk to me."

Her husband didn't respond. The night kept quiet save for the distant chirp of chatty crickets. As she got closer to the doorway, she heard a noise sounding a lot like displaced air, whispers of an invisible something moving across the room. Her brain immediately likened the sound to a baseball bat swinging through a fastball, the sound of lumber making contact with nothing but the still atmosphere. The noise grew louder as she crept closer.

"Terry?" she asked the blazing blue light again, this time in a voice barely above a whisper. She touched the door with her fingertips and forced it inward, being careful not to linger; her ruined palm reminded her to be quick.

The door gave way to a confusing scene. The room was hardly the same one she'd left to go fetch a glass of water. It was drenched in neon blue light and nothing else. Her bed, her dresser, the nightstand, and the small forty-inch television were all gone, replaced by a soft, tumbling mist that filled the room. Dreamily, Angela drifted into the room, letting the coils of fog roll over her. The roiling clouds curled and twisted around her body like an anaconda.

Then, as if coming from another room in the house, someone screamed. Angela's heart momentarily stopped, her breath catching in her throat. She tried calling out for her husband but she was voiceless. The realization that this was not a dream stole her words away. Terry cried out again, this one louder than the last. Angela felt tears trickling down her cheeks. Her veins were rivers of ice. Bumps broke out across her flesh as a haunting tickle danced on her nape. She turned to the door but it was shut now, the handle glowing molten red, the button in the center pushed to indicate *someone* had locked her in.

Someone. Something.

Some unseen thing.

Whatever the presence was, it waited in there with her. And it didn't want her to leave.

From somewhere off in the distance, Terry screamed again. The inarticulate call for help seemed several houses away.

How was this possible? She'd gone downstairs fifteen minutes ago. *How could this happen so quickly?*

She was hallucinating again. There was no other explanation for the cobalt scenery, at least nothing logical. She needed to ride this waking nightmare out until Terry came to her rescue and towed her out, lugged her back to reality.

But that scream.

His scream.

It sounded so real.

And so far away.

She had no choice. Moving into the mist, drifting along with the tumbling waves of fog, she concentrated on the invisible course she had set, toward the bed. The bathroom door was next to it, and she figured, *if* she could reach the threshold safely, she could crawl out the window, onto the roof, and figure out what to do next once she got there.

Deeper into the cerulean mist, she traveled. A few steps in, she glanced back over her shoulder and saw the door was gone, enveloped in tufts of foggy barricades. A part of her, the rational half, the part which hadn't lost itself in her own delusions, realized this couldn't be real. That this wasn't a hallucination; it was a living nightmare. That she was currently in bed, her overactive imagination dealing her a doozy of a dream. She convinced herself she'd fallen asleep and soon she'd wake to her little slice of American Pie, next to her loving husband who'd shower her with hugs and kisses and morning cuddles. But then she peered down at the fleshy ruin that was her palm and her mind suddenly went to dark places, allowing the other part of her— the sinister half—to speculate. This part of her persuaded her to believe she lived in a bewitched house, that this was a product of the woman who had lived here for two months, hexing the place, spreading her witchcraft throughout every room, casting spells on every material thing she owned. She directed her attention back to the blanket of blue fog before her, the direction of the path to the bathroom, and raced toward the threshold.

What should have been a three-second march turned into a thirty-second hike, and she was no closer to the bathroom than she had been half a minute ago. There were no doors ahead—just an endless stretch of turbulent brume.

Impossible.

But was it? Was it any more impossible than peering through a hole in her bathroom wall and witnessing a tiny pirate ship suffer destruction under the beastly force of an enormous Kraken? Or being the only person on the planet tuning into *Let's Switch Houses!* that saw the old woman conducting some sort of sinister séance in her living room? What about the dream she'd experienced? The one where her house sat in the middle of a place known only to her as The Everywhere, though, she had no clue how or why she knew it was called that. That was when dreams were just dreams and they were allowed to be nonsense. Now she had different opinions on dreams and how they should behave.

She longed for the days when dreams were just dreams and not horrible realities.

Ignoring her thoughts and the hopelessness they tacked on her shoulders, she surged ahead, pushing her way through the mist. The acrid stench that had made her want to revisit her dinner grew bolder. The sound of air whooshing past her ear became distinct, louder. Almost *inside* her ear. Like a ball pitched at her head, missing by mere inches.

A shadow materialized in the mist. A figure. A man or a woman, she couldn't tell which. Whoever (*whatever*) it was acted as if they were dancing, frolicking in the blue haze overlaying the bedroom.

If this is still my bedroom, she thought irrationally. She couldn't shake the feeling that her body and mind were somewhere else now, lost in a place between places.

(The Everywhere)

(Ma-me)

The figure bumped into her, knocking her back a few feet. Upon closer inspection, she realized the phantom-like being was a man, and he was naked, his body taking on the same hue as the rest of the room, that cobalt glow. His back faced her and his arms were moving as if entwined in some Egyptian boogie, mimicking the flow of octopus tentacles waving through the depths of the ocean. His limbs moved awkwardly as if he were double or triple-jointed. The unsettling fluidity of his movements made her instantly nauseous, and she felt stomach bile burn her throat upon its ascent.

Then, the figure turned and faced her.

Her heart hammered, slamming against her chest cage.

Both of the figure's eyes and mouth were sewn shut, black wire laced up over them, the healing wounds oozing with infection. The man whimpered, or maybe laughed—Angela couldn't tell which—and then disappeared as rolls of fog draped over him. She watched his shadow dance into nothingness.

Angela shrieked, but her voice received no echo, no play anywhere except the few feet in front of her mouth. The dense mist smothered her sound, absorbing the echo of her shrill outburst.

Another figure appeared; this one female. She was also naked, walking slowly as if she'd died and reanimated. Exiting the mist, the unclothed woman entered a small clearing about three feet from Angela. Her mouth and eyes were also wired shut. Dribbles of blood ran from the incisions, leaking down her cheeks and the sides of her face. She stumbled past Angela, paying no attention to anything except whatever she was striding toward. Angela kept completely still and clapped her hand over her mouth, careful not to utter a single noise.

Where am I? she thought as thick loops of fog swallowed up the woman's shadow. *What is this place?* It certainly wasn't home and certainly wasn't Red River, New Jersey. Once, when she was about nine, she'd gotten lost, turned around, in the woods near her parents' home. Every path looked the same, every tree. It had taken her hours to wander her way out. The dread of becoming lost, coupled with the plausible possibility she'd never be found, was a unique experience, one she thought she'd never feel again. But now, in the place that wasn't her bedroom and likely wasn't *anywhere*, that odd sense of being misplaced nestled against her bones once again.

She continued on, mindful of the shadows forming at the edge of obscurity. A few more naked shufflers scurried past, some more grotesque than others. Some of the walking corpses wore zippers on their flesh, the kind found on puffy snow jackets. One gentleman cruised by, opening the zipper across his stomach as he passed Angela, letting everything inside tumble out onto the floor. To Angela, the spilled contents looked like a heap of uncooked meats mixed with a few jars of chunky tomato sauce. She avoided contact by simply dodging past, preventing her curious eyes from wandering. The man didn't follow her but his head spun in her direction as she skipped by. She felt his eyes—not that he had any—on the back of her neck until she had made it far enough into the mist to where she felt safe.

She walked for ten minutes. More of the shambling dead came and went; each one eager to show her things that brought forth disgust and bouts of nausea, things she couldn't possibly conjure on her own. A man walked by with a hacksaw blade halfway buried in his throat, and he was hellbent on working the fine-toothed metal all the way through, streams of blood pouring from the ragged slice. A woman plucked her own fingernails off with her teeth, laughing hysterically as each one tore free. Two children were dragging a toy behind them, tugging on a piece of rope, only it took a moment for Angela to notice the toy was an adult (possibly a parent) and the long rope was the man's intestines. They skipped happily off into the mist, reciting some nursery rhyme in a language foreign to Angela's ears.

She tried to close her eyes and blind herself to all these horrible events, but found she had zero control over that part of her face. Some unnamed force had pinned her eyelids open, compelling her to engage in the horrors before her.

It's a dream, she thought. *This is one majorly fucked-up nightmare and soon you'll wake and this bullshit will all be over.*

But the flitting horrors didn't feel like a dream, not entirely. They appeared as real as anything she'd ever experienced.

She heard her husband scream, again. Closer this time. Real close. As if he were only ten yards away.

The haze grew thicker, devouring the last remaining shred of clarity. Flashes of lightning, those bright blinding bursts, quickened their pace, narrowing the downtime between appearances. The smell, those nose-wrenching fumes, intensified.

Through the swirling haze, she made out another figure, a man lacking a single garment. The room's newest victim was stretched, each of his four limbs pulled taut as if about to be quartered.

The man was her husband.

"Terry!" she shouted, rushing ahead without caution.

Her husband tried to respond, but no words made it past his sewn lips. He'd been stripped naked and all of his body hair—including what little remained on the top of his head—had been shaved. She glanced down at his genitals to find them gone, replaced by an open, bleeding cavity that supplied the ground with steady droplets of dark crimson.

She screamed in horror.

Terry screamed, too. Although his eyes were glued shut, tears still leaked through, basking his face in a heavily glistening sheen. He tried to move, squirm free, but his wrists and ankles were bound by barbed wire.

She approached him slowly, her vision blurry from the gush of tears flooding her eyes.

The closer she got, the tighter the wire twisted around his flesh. The more he screamed. The more the lightning flashed and the more turbulent the room of clouds grew.

She stopped. Dropped to her knees.

"Terry?" she asked, throwing her head in her hands. "What is happening to us? What is this place?"

He shouted, but his sewn mouth trapped the words and only produced nonsense. She didn't understand a single syllable. She cried some more, and he screamed some more.

Without warning, the black wire attached to his limbs snapped, pulling Terry apart. Each of his appendages tore free from his body and disappeared somewhere into the surrounding realm, leaving crimson torrents in its wake. Blood exploded from the fresh scarlet pits like a city fire hydrant in the dead heat of summer.

Wet crimson splashed across her face. Its warmth coated her flesh, and the sickening sensation caused her to vomit and urinate simultaneously. She screamed and screamed, and screamed some more, until—

When she removed her hands from her face, the bright early morning greeted her with open, loving arms. A square of light coming in through the kitchen window nearly blinded her. Birds chirped right outside the window, perhaps while removing pine needles and leaves from the gutter to build their late-season nests. She checked the immediate area for evidence of what she'd witnessed, but there wasn't any—no Terry, no puddles of blood, no blue light, no active fog, nothing of the sort. Her knees felt wobbly as she pushed to her feet. When she walked, the tile floor of the kitchen shifted beneath her.

She used the counter to guide herself to the other side of the room, where she lingered in the doorway between the kitchen and the living room.

How did I get here?

The last thing she remembered was wandering aimlessly in the blue fog blanketing her bedroom; now, she found herself in the kitchen, basking in the early morning sunlight. She checked her palm, the one seared by the ultra-hot doorknob. It appeared fine, her hand clean and unmarked, the skin perfect and smooth, zero evidence of her terrible ordeal ever having happened.

Holy shit, what the hell is happening to me? Angela thought as the room spun in all different directions. She felt ill. Really ill. She forgot about the floor and its shiftiness, and rushed across the kitchen toward the sink. She arrived just in time; remnants of what she had eaten the night before came back up and layered the bottom of the sink.

"Oh, God." After she finished unloading and felt depleted of all fluids, she reached across the counter and grabbed her pills, the new prescription Dr. Wilson had filled for her. She popped a pill, poured herself a small glass of tap water, and swallowed her medicine. *This better start working soon,* she thought, *before I lose what's left of my sanity.* She decided she'd call Abbie later and ask her how long the pills should take to work their magic. She'd taken one dose yesterday and, yet, she had just experienced the most intense delusion of this whole ordeal.

Her phone buzzed in her pocket. She looked down and saw her husband's name with the word "work" next to it, the auto body shop's number beneath them.

"Hey," she answered.

"Hey, babe," he said. "How's my favorite wife?"

She swallowed and it felt like the pill she had ingested was lodged in her throat. *Don't tell him,* her inner voice urged. *Don't tell him.*

"I'm... I'm actually doing okay."

"That's great. Really great to hear." He paused. In the background, she heard his co-workers laughing at a joke she hadn't caught the beginning of. "No nightmares last night?"

"Um, no. Why do you ask?"

"I don't know. I thought I heard you moving around a lot. Just wondering if you were okay."

"Did I wake you?"

"No—I mean, yeah. Once. But it wasn't a big deal. I went right back to sleep." He waited as if he knew she had something to admit. "You sure you're okay?"

"Yeah, fine."

"You sure? You don't sound okay?"

"I am. I just… woke up feeling a little ill."

"Sick?"

"Maybe."

"Well, stay home and get some rest today. Don't leave the couch unless you need to use the bathroom or eat something." Playfully, he said, "Husband's orders."

"Actually, I was thinking about taking a ride to visit my parents."

"Really?" He sounded surprised. "Without me?"

She laughed. "Like you care. What did you call them the last time you were there? Bloodsucking gremlins?"

"That sounds about right. Look, I'm fine with it, as long as you're truly okay. Do you think it's a good idea, being sick and all?"

"I'm actually feeling much better already. I'm super hungry. I think I just need some breakfast and I'll be good to go."

"Okay, babe. Keep in touch. Drive carefully. You know the drill. Call me when you get there." In the background, someone called Terry's name. "Gotta go, love. Will you be home for dinner?"

"Depends. You know what long drives do to me. I'm considering staying over."

"Really?"

"Yeah, I mean, if it's okay with you."

Terry paused. "Yeah. It's… it's fine."

"Okay."

"I'll hang out with the guys tonight."

"Okay."

"Text me, though?"

"Of course."

"Love you."

"Love you, too."

VII.

THE CONFESSION OF ROSALYN JEFFRIES

She felt guilty about lying to Terry, especially during those few seconds when her parents' exit on the Garden State Parkway zipped past, but it had to be done. She couldn't tell him she was skipping a nice dinner and perhaps another majestic night of intimacy in favor of seeking out the old woman, the old witch whom she was pretty sure was out to kill her, or, at the very least, trying to break down what little remained of her sanity. She couldn't tell him because he couldn't possibly understand what she'd been through. Everything from the day it had all gone down, the moment *[we do not speak his name]* vanished up until her experience on the *Switch!,* had been pure hell. Terry didn't bear the same burdens; therefore, he could never understand her guilt, her agony, her mental exhaustion. All that, plus, any excuse to get away from the house was a good one.

That cursed place.

The woman had said, *If you think you need help, please seek me out.* Help. Of that, Angela needed plenty.

During the drive, she replayed the woman's generous offer over in her head. Angela didn't exactly know what to make of it. If the woman was trying to assassinate her, offering help was hardly the traditional approach. Or was it?

Maybe it's a trap? All part of her little mind game. To break me down. Make me see shit that isn't there, then build me up with empty promises. Only to take it all away again.

Her mind began to work against her, conjuring up ways to fit all the misshapen pieces into the complex puzzle that had become her life. *Maybe she can't enter the house on Trenton Road. Maybe she needs me to come to her. Maybe it's all part of her twisted design.*

Or maybe just the opposite. Maybe the woman *wasn't* trying to kill her. Maybe the house itself sought violence, maybe because of what had happened there. What she did to *[we do not speak his name]*. Maybe her actions opened a locked door, let in whatever was waiting on the other side.

No. Impossible.

Maybe she's just trying to help.

She thought she'd phone Barry on the way to, number one—question him about Rosalyn, and number two—help pass the time. The six-hour drive to the Vermont border would be long and boring, and Angela hated long, boring drives. She called Barry but the prick didn't answer. An hour later, he called back.

"What's up, superstar?"

"Oh stop."

"What? You're going to be a household name in a few short weeks. Guaranteed." And she would, only not in the way Barry Harrison intended. "So… what can I do for you, sweetie-pie?"

"I'd like to know more about the woman who stayed in our house."

A brief silence lingered. "Rosalyn Jeffries?"

"Yes. Her."

"Why?" Is everything all right? She didn't, like, do anything to the house, did she?"

Angela's breath caught in her throat.

"Angela?"

"Yes?"

"Why do you want to know about Rosalyn?"

"I don't know."

"Come on. Don't be coy with me. Tell me. I thought we were buddies?"

"We are. We are."

"Then tell me."

Frustrated, she growled. "It's just the house, man. The house is weird. I'm getting super strange vibes from it."

"Okay. That's it?"

"Yeah. Isn't that enough?" She suddenly grew suspicious of her former producer. He acted like he knew something but he wanted to know what Angela knew before spilling the whole story. "What do you know, Barry?"

"I know nothing."

"You don't sound like you know nothing."

"What do you want to know, Angela?"

"The woman. What's her deal?"

It was Barry's turn to exhaust a breath of frustration. "She's just some nutty old woman we chose to be on the show, okay. That's it. She lost her husband a few months back, around the same time as…you know," *[we do not speak his name],* "and we thought it'd be a good match. She was a little odd on set. She kept rambling on about a bad aura, how her husband's ghost wouldn't show himself there, and some other crazy shit that's going to make for some kick-ass television."

"Whoa, whoa. Slow down. Her husband's ghost wouldn't *show himself* there?" Her brow climbed to the top of her forehead. "What the hell does that mean?"

"Yeah, her words, hon. Not mine."

Angela shook her head as she passed the big, green LEAVING NEW JERSEY sign. "I don't like that, Barry. You should have told me."

Another pause. "Did you… do you know?"

She didn't like the smallness of his voice. "Know what?"

"Nothing. Never mind."

"Barry?" She grunted with heated frustration. "What do you need to tell me?"

The producer sighed, filling her ear with static. "Okay, look. Promise you won't be mad."

"Why don't you tell me and I'll decide if it's worth getting mad over."

"Okay. Here it goes. I did some research on Rosalyn Jeffries. After we got her into your house, I got weirded out by her. You know, like I said, she was talking about some wild stuff. She was obsessed with the supernatural, spirits and demons, and, for whatever reason, she was convinced something wicked was taking place on Trenton Road. Something sinister. I believe her exact words were 'corrupted shadows', or something like that. Now that I mention it, a lot of what happened there is kind of foggy."

Angela noticed how hard she was gripping the steering wheel; color had bled from her knuckles, rendering them a row of eight white bumps.

"Anyway, I did my research."

"After you hired her?"

Barry clicked his tongue. "We did a background check prior, but nothing came up. Honest, Angela, if I had known, there was no way we would have put her on *Switch!* I want you to know that."

Angela's neck constricted, every muscle, from her chin down, tightening like a screw. "What did she do, Barry?"

"Angela…"

"WHAT DID SHE DO?" she screamed into the phone. Her car swerved, nearly side-swiping the maroon van next to her. The man in the vehicle honked his horn, rolled down his window so he could shout obscenities, and capped his tirade off with a middle-fingered salute. Angela smiled at him and returned her attention back to the road. She found a calm place in her mind and huddled there. Her nerves simmered. "What did she do?" she asked again, softly this time.

"According to Google, Rosalyn Jeffries got mixed up in some local cult back in the sixties. I guess you could call it a coven, a group of witches. The only reason there was any documentation of this cult—called *The Sisterhood of Sin*, in case you wanted to know—was because in '68, one of their members died. A woman. She was found all burnt up, head to toe. Baked to a crisp. There was an investigation, according to the article, but nothing was ever done. No charges were brought against any of the members, especially their leader, a woman by the name of Ester Moore."

Barry stopped, and the big man's heavy breaths filled her ear.

"What else?" she asked, clearly irritated.

"That's it. Honest. I wouldn't have even found anything if it weren't for her picture and the caption citing her name."

"A Google search. After she signed on for the show."

"I had to dig deep, Angela. This wasn't the first hit, mind you. I think the article was on the twelfth page. Don't ask me why I went beyond the first couple." She heard him swallow and sensed he was on the verge of tears. She could tell this situation was eating away at him, and, though she probably had every right to, she wouldn't press him. "I just felt something off…"

"Barry, want some advice?"

"Sure…" he said, his voice strained.

"Fire your investigators. They suck ass."

She hung up. Next, she dialed Abbie. Her psychiatrist picked up on the first ring.

"Angela? I wasn't expecting to hear from you so soon. How are you feeling? Is everything all right?"

"Eh, I've been better." She proceeded to tell her about Barry's confession. "I know. Crazy stuff. But it could explain a lot about what I'm experiencing lately." She opened her mouth, but realized what she was about to say and who she was about to say it to.

"Angela, these manifestations. They aren't real, sweetheart."

"I know. I just… I don't know what I just said. I know how insane that sounded. I'm sorry."

"Don't apologize. It's fine. You're just confused. Look, why don't you drop by the office later. I can clear my afternoon and—"

"I can't."

"Why not?" She almost sounded insulted.

"Because…"

"Angela?"

"Because I'm on my way to Vermont."

"Vermont? But, why—" Abbie stopped herself. "Angela, what are you thinking about doing?"

"I… I don't know exactly."

"As your psychiatrist, I must say, this is a terrible idea. I'm all for confronting your fears and dealing with roadblocks, but in a natural, controlled environment. When the patient pushes the issue—"

"To hell with your psycho-babble-bullshit."

Silence. *That finally shut her up.*

"I'm sorry," Angela said. "Look, your pills aren't fucking working, okay. The other night I walked through hell, literally *hell*, and I saw things I *never* want to see again. So unless you give me something that works right now, right *fucking* now, or hand over some sage-like advice that will make all this bad shit go away, make the last nine months of my fucking life disa-fucking-ppear, then I'm taking things into my own hands."

She waited, but Abbie kept silent.

"I didn't think so."

"Angela, I feel sorry for you. I really do. You're deeply troubled and you don't know what you're doing. You need help. I'm thinking a full psychiatric evaluation in a controlled environment. I know a great place within twenty miles of here—"

"I'm not checking myself into a fucking mental ward!" She was hyperventilating now. Her erratic driving earned her honks from her highway neighbors. More middle fingers were flipped her way, and she ignored every single one of them. When she thought there was no more air left in her lungs, she careened her car over to the side of the road, where she stopped and shut off the engine.

"I think you need to come in, Angela. This is clearly out of your hands. We need to escalate things. Get you better before you do something to harm yourself or others."

Angela planted her face in her hands and cried, heaving sobs. Her palms grew slick with tears.

"Think about what Terry would want."

She lifted her head. "Abbie. I'm going to Vermont. I'm going to talk with Rosalyn Jeffries, and I'm going to find out exactly what the fuck she did to my house."

"I think that's a very poor decision, but it's your life, dear."

"That's right. It's my life," she said, though it hadn't felt like hers for quite some time. "It's my life and I'm going to do what I want. For me."

"Can I—"

She ended the call.

After she gathered herself, stopped crying and patted her face dry on the sleeve of her shirt, she pulled back onto the parkway and merged with traffic.

She stopped three more times, each so she could vomit.

The phone sat on the desk, staring up at her. It didn't take long after the last call to decide what came next. Picking up the phone, she punched in the name and hit "SEND."

She waited.

Three rings.

"What?" the gruff voice answered.

"It's time," the woman said.

Silence hung on the line. Then: "Are you sure?"

"The plan is in motion. We need to act now."

"Is the child in danger?"

"No. Not yet. But if we don't hurry…"

"I'll leave now."

"Good. If you hurry, you just might make it."

"I'll call you when it's done."

"See that you do."

She slammed down the phone, leaned back in her chair, and became lost in the painting on the far wall, the one with a vase full of dead, black roses.

She parked at the end of the cul-de-sac, near the main road, got out, and walked the rest of the way. There weren't many houses on Boulder Court, three in total, and the Jeffries' house was the only one facing the highway, as the others were stuck fronting each other. She scurried down the sidewalk, toward the house she had recently spent two long months in. She didn't know why she wanted to stroll down the block but felt it had something to do with her and her husband's after-dinner routine, their nightly lap around the development to take in the New England scenery. She took a breath of fresh air and compared it to Red River's; it was no contest—the Vermont air was fresher, sweeter, always accompanied by a hint of smoked hickory. To Angela, the air back home was stale and dry, hardly something to take a moment to appreciate. The atmosphere was often tainted with heavy motor pollution and street trash.

Reaching the woman's cement porch, she jogged up the stone steps, one at a time, briskly. She knocked on the door and received no answer. She knocked again, this time looking at the curtain covering the bay window next to the door, anticipating the slightest flicker of movement. But there was nothing. She knocked a third time, rang the doorbell, and peeked through the semi-transparent curtain, but she saw no shadows or silhouettes moving behind it, only darkness with the faint glow of the afternoon sun beaming through the kitchen window opposite the main living space.

She decided to try something else.

Angela jogged down the stoop, toward the garage. She peeked around the neighborhood, making sure the nosy neighbors weren't studying her from their windows, eyeing her every move. She didn't notice any spies and shook off the notion that she was being watched.

She ducked under the overhang and approached the garage door. Flipping up the cover on the keypad, she recalled the combination she and Terry had used many times before. She punched in the digits and frowned when the garage door failed to rise.

Shit, she thought, *she changed the combo.*

She wasn't surprised.

No matter—she knew the key to the backdoor was under the welcome mat. There was no way the woman changed all the locks in her house, not yet. Why would she? Angela and Terry had decided they weren't going to swap out their locks back home, but, after considering current events, she thought they might have to reconsider.

Maybe she had done the same.

Angela jogged around the side of the house, unlatched the small hip-high gate, walked around the property until the back deck, composite and stained with a color the company called Foggy Island, was in view. She streaked toward the platform, bounding the steps two at a time, and dashed over to the back door. Bending down, she glanced over her shoulder, expecting to see the old woman at the edge of the deck, arms folded and tapping her foot as if she'd caught her grandson's hand in the cookie jar. But there was no one there, nothing but the lush green forest beyond the property line.

She was alone. And that fact comforted her.

She grabbed the key, slipped it into the lock, and popped open the door. Before barging in, she poked her head in the kitchen and called the old woman. "Mrs. Jeffries?"

No answer. The interior sat in still, silent shadows.

All right then. Let's do this.

She crossed the threshold and stepped onto the linoleum floor, closing the door behind her. Bypassing the light switch, opting for security the shadows provided, she trekked across the kitchen, into the living room. She headed for the bay window and peeked out. Still no car in the driveway. The woman was not here. She had beaten her home, which didn't seem possible unless the woman either drove ten miles per hour under the speed limit or stopped several more times than she had. Either was likely, she supposed.

Or maybe she's still stalking me in Red River, Angela thought.

Seek me out, the woman had said.

No, she's on her way back. She has to be.

Angela decided she'd wait for her. But, while she waited, she figured she'd have herself a look around.

After dawdling around downstairs, Angela made her way to the second floor, heading directly for the bedroom. When she reached the bedroom door, she felt different. Scared. Like she wasn't supposed to be here, like she didn't belong. Much like she had in her *own* house lately, that harrowing sensation of being lost in familiar places. A sense of dread pulled at the hairs on her neck. Her stomach swirled like a renegade tornado. A dull throb kicked around her eardrums.

In the entire two months she'd spent there, she had never felt that way.

An unrecognizable odor reached her nostrils, the unpleasantness causing her stomach to swell with nausea. Pressure built up in her sinuses, forcing her to squint. She fought through it and pushed open the door, revealing the madness inside.

The smell nearly caused her to faint. The pungency bowled into her like some palpable thing, pushing her back, pressing her spine against the wall in the hallway. The room reeked of rotten meats and sun-spoiled dairy. She turned her head and retched. Slipping the collar of her shirt over her nose (not that it helped block the odor), she headed into the bedroom. The putrid stench was so fierce her eyes began to water. Surveying the corners of the room, she quickly detected what was causing the horrendous odor.

Dead chickens.

Three of them. On the dresser, the headless sacks of feathers lay casually as if they were a stack of mail or some other ordinary household clutter. A collection of flies hovered over the carcasses, buzzing with delight. She avoided eye contact with the savage display, hoping the less she saw, the less she would smell. But that wasn't the case. As she focused her attention on something other than the raw flyblown meat, the smell remained just as bold.

The condition of the walls seized her vision next; they were once painted almond, but now held dark tones, and engraved in the sheetrock were symbols, the same exact insignias she'd seen during the season premiere of *Switch!* Circles over triangles, fused with ellipses and hexagons.

Various combinations of symbols holding no distinguishable meaning, at least not to her.

Droplets of blood speckled the carpet.

Dreamcatchers hung from the ceiling like party streamers at some five-year-old's birthday party.

A bloody blade lay in the center of the bed. Crimson soaked the comforter.

Whose blood is that? she began to wonder, and her eyes drifted back across the room, over to the dresser where the headless chickens continued to serve as snack food for a horde of busy insects.

Before she moved into the master bathroom, her eyes ran over the walls, taking in every elegant detail of the scrawled shapes.

"I've been praying day and night," a voice said from behind her.

Angela spun so fast she nearly lost her footing. Clutching onto the bedposts, she sucked in her scream. She tried to yell, but her voice died, fear killing the words as they entered her throat.

"Hush, child," the old woman said, placing her free hand on her chin, extending one finger and resting it on her lips. "Don't be frightened. You have no need to be scared."

Angela begged to differ. The chill currently crawling over her flesh, trespassing to various parts of her anatomy, sang a different song.

"At least," Rosalyn Jeffries started to say, looking down at the bag full of dead chickens in her other hand, "at least, not of me."

For the moment, the chickens still had their heads.

Rosalyn set a mug full of something dark down in front of her, the broth murky like a bold-roast coffee. Angela breathed in the steam, inhaling the herbal scent wafting up from the unknown liquid.

"It's tea," Rosalyn said reassuringly. "A very special blend."

She lost most of her thirst at "special blend" but Angela decided to drink it anyway. If the woman's plan was to kill her, surely there were more direct approaches. She sipped slowly as Rosalyn set herself down on the chair across from her.

"It's good," Angela said, licking her lips, savoring the nutty aftertaste.

"Thank you." Rosalyn looked at her, smiling. "I'm so glad you're here."

"Why *am* I here, Rosalyn?" Angela didn't return the smile. She stared into the woman's eyes, unblinking.

"You're not one to beat around the bush, are you?" She nodded. "All right, all right. Let's get down to it."

Angela couldn't place the woman's accent, not exactly. Definitely European. German or Austrian, if she had to guess. "Where are you from, Rosalyn?"

"Me? America, sweetheart. My parents were from Germany. I grew up speaking their language. If you're wondering about my accent, it's because—yes, English is my second tongue."

"I didn't mean to offend."

The old woman raised her palms. "No offense taken! I'm proud of my heritage." She must have noticed the uninterested look in her guest's eyes because her expression faded. "But you didn't come here to talk about my roots, did you?"

"No, Rosalyn. I did not."

"Well, then. I guess I should ask—how much do you know about what's happening on 44 Trenton Road in Red River, New Jersey?"

Angela shrugged. "Not much. Other than I'm seeing a whole lot of freaky shit that isn't really there."

Rosalyn nodded as if she shared a common problem. "Tell me, sweetheart," she said, glancing down at the table where she traced circles with her finger. "Have you ever heard of something called a Mare?"

"A Mare?"

The woman nodded.

Angela shook her head. "No, I can't say I have. Unless you mean an old horse?"

Rosalyn didn't speak.

"Or a night-*mare.*"

The old woman looked up from the table, her expression dead still. "That's precisely where they got their names from." The corner of her mouth pulled slightly, the faintest evidence of a smirk. "Or rather, nightmares got their name from them."

"Them?"

"Mares. They have many other names. Alps. Sleep demons. I prefer to call them what they truly are—*dream goblins.*"

Angela stared at the woman, her eyebrows stretching as high as they would go. "Oh-kay then." She stood up from the kitchen table, sliding the chair across the linoleum floor, making a loud scraping noise that caused both women to cringe.

"Where are you going?" Rosalyn asked, squinting at her guest.

"Far, far away from here."

Rosalyn pushed herself to her feet. "Nonsense, child. You are in terrible danger."

"Because of dream goblins?" She scoffed. "Do you know how goddamn ridiculous that sounds?"

"Ridiculous or not, that is what I believe has marked your home. A Mare is an ancient creature, a demon of sorts, that latches onto a certain individual and tortures them by infiltrating their dreams, manipulating them until their mind can no longer bear the horrific images, until there's nothing left of the victim's sanity. Then... it takes what it wants. In this case, Mrs. Shepard, I believe what it wants is your home. And something else..." The old woman's face became long, drawn with worry. "It chooses victims who have experienced some sort of tragedy."

[we do not speak his name]

Raising her chin, the old woman gulped. "Those who have gone through terrible ordeals make it easier for the goblins to access their dreams. They're more susceptible to this kind of, what I'd like to call, *possession.*"

"This is crazy."

"Hard to believe, yes." Rosalyn offered what looked like a comforting smile. "But not crazy. I knew something was amiss the second I stepped foot in your house. I felt it wash over me, an incredible wave of perpetual evil. I haven't felt intense power like that since... well, since a very long time ago."

"Like, say... since 1968?" The question came out sharp, with more venom than Angela desired.

The woman didn't seem fazed, her expression hardly changing. "I assume Barry told you about his discovery. Yes, it's true. All of it."

"You killed a woman."

There was a pause. Rosalyn Jeffries sat completely still.

"Oh my God," Angela said, covering her mouth with her hand.

"She didn't die by my hand, but by another. I was there. The woman's death hangs over me every day I open my eyes."

"Did your husband know?"

"I told my husband everything. Much like I assume you do. Or did. Before…"

"How did he take the news?"

Rosalyn's eyes darted across the room, as if something had flashed in her periphery, then settled her vision back on her guest. Angela followed the old woman's gaze to the corner of the kitchen, but saw nothing.

"My husband has forgiven me for my past, the decisions I made when I was a young, stupid girl." She reached her hands across the table, palms up, asking Angela for hers. "I'm asking you to do the same, Angela Shepard. You and your husband's lives depend on it."

Slowly, Angela planted herself back in the chair. She didn't offer her hands to the old woman.

Rosalyn cleared her throat. "Mrs. Shepard, please. Do not make the same mistakes I have."

"Same mistakes?" Angela laughed incredulously. "I have no intentions of killing any—"

"Forget that. That's not what I'm talking about."

"Then what are you talking about?"

"Do not let yourself ignore the signs before you." Her eyes filled with water, glistening in the dim light the overhead bulbs provided. Those surging tears were the only thing keeping Angela seated, preventing her from fleeing the house, screaming for the entire neighborhood to hear. The woman's story, impossible as it sounded, felt authentic. Angela was surprised to find herself buying into Rosalyn's tale.

Sort of.

Not quite.

It can't be real.

But something in the back of her mind said differently.

It's all real. All of it. The dream goblins. They've marked you. They're coming to get you. First your dreams. Then your reality.

"My husband, Carl," Rosalyn began, blotting her eyes with a napkin. "He was… he was in terrible danger. Much like yourself. He had something chasing him, following him night after night. I sensed it somewhere in the distance, somewhere hidden in the darkest regions of the netherworld. Even though I haven't practiced in years, I'm still connected to the darkness, the places where light doesn't dare go.

Something was following him, all right; I sensed the foul spirit the way a rabbit senses a sneaking wolf. The creature was good and clever, always kept dodging my eye. The blasted thing covered its tracks well, leaving no traces of its existence behind. I couldn't find it. I searched the darkest places, points on the celestial map I haven't trespassed in years, and I came up empty. Carl told me he was fine and not to worry, whatever it was would pass, but I knew better. I knew the thing was persistent and desperate to have him. But, like a good, obedient wife, I listened to him." She sniffled as more tears streamed down her face. "But I shouldn't have. I should have persisted. I shouldn't have ignored the signs. The evidence. I... I let that thing kill my husband, Mrs. Shepard. All because I was too complacent."

Angela shook her head. "You said on television he died of a heart attack."

"Yes, well, who would believe me if I said he had been stalked and killed by some unspeakable evil?"

"I don't know. Maybe the same amount of people who believed you when you said he visits you nightly. Maybe about that many?"

"People believe in communication with the other side, Mrs. Shepard. A recent national poll showed that last year forty-two percent of Americans believed in supernatural entities. In Europe, it's well over fifty."

Angela closed her eyes and bit her bottom lip. "That doesn't make it true."

"No, but as someone who has tampered with the darkness, who has harnessed certain energies invisible to the naked eye, I can assure you, Mrs. Shepard—it's all true."

"Well, I haven't seen a shred of evidence other than what's been going on in my house. And that's just me losing my fucking mind." The woman's eyes bulged. "Pardon my French."

She ignored the foul language. "You need to believe me."

"Whatever is happening, Rosalyn, it isn't supernatural. It's just a product of what happened over eight months ago. It's me."

"In a way, you are correct, Mrs. Shepard. It is about what happened to *[we do not speak his name]*. The tragedy. These monsters thrive on it. Feed on those negative emotions like vampires to an open wound."

Angela snarled at the old woman. "How dare you," she barked.

Rosalyn recoiled as if she'd been slapped. "How dare I what?"

"Speak his name. You have no right."

Rosalyn twirled her hands in the air. "I don't mean to be disrespectful. I only want to help you."

Angela's eyes traveled up the stairs. She pointed to the area of the house where she thought the master bedroom was, where the pile of dead chickens rested on the bureau. "By sacrificing chickens? Cutting off their fucking heads? I'm starting to see who the crazy one is here, and I'm starting to think it's not me."

The old woman shook her head. "It was an old ritual to keep the dream goblins out. I thought it would help."

"Enough with the dream goblin shit!"

"Mrs. Shepard, you and your husband are in grave danger."

"Yeah, so you've said."

"I've been trying to warn you. Reach you. You need to stay away from that house. You need to stay away from Red River altogether. Your son…"

Angela's eyes grew with rage. "Watch your tongue, woman…" she said venomously.

"Your son. He isn't dead."

Angela's heart stopped. The air in the room instantly died. For a second, the world around her did not exist. She recalled the pharmacist's assistant and what Angela thought she'd heard her say: *He's still alive… in your heart.* She got the sense that that wasn't what she'd meant, that the second half of her uninvited opinion was only a cover-up for the first.

"How *dare* you say that to me."

"Mrs. Shepard, please. It's holding him. The dream goblin has him in the Everywhere and it won't let go until he has you… and the life inside your belly."

Angela felt her heart skip, stop, and take a full five seconds to start pumping again. "What the hell did you just say to me?"

"You don't know?"

Her mouth went dry. She could barely speak the word, "No."

"You're pregnant. Only a few weeks. Haven't you been feeling unwell?"

She recalled the three barf sessions on the way up here. "I thought…" Her eyes fluttered. The room began to slide like a carnival funhouse trick. She thought she might be sick again. "I thought that was…"

"You're pregnant, Mrs. Shepard. It's the other thing the dream goblin wants. Your unborn child."

"But how?" She swallowed what felt like a pebble. "I'm on the pill."

"Hardly a miracle, I'm guessing. Something tells me someone has been messing with your medication."

Angela shook her head. *Medication. The pharmacist's assistant.*

She immediately went for her purse and rummaged around for the prescription bottle. Once she located it, she removed it and quickly scanned the label for its litany of warnings. "May render birth control pills ineffective," she read, and with the words, her heart plummeted. "Son of a bitch."

"The dream goblin's reach extends beyond the dream world, I'm afraid." The old woman's eyes narrowed. "It may exist in the Everywhere, but it has agents. Right now, it's trapped there. But it's chosen you, marked you, to be its carrier."

"Carrier?"

"It wants to become you, Mrs. Shepard. That's all these creatures ever want—a way out of their world and into ours."

Angela closed her eyes. "Why me?"

"Maybe because you lost *him.*"

Seething, Angela shot her a warning glance.

"Maybe because you lost yourself," Rosalyn added. "I know what I say angers you. And it should. But know this—I am not filling your head with falsehoods. What I say is the truth. All of it. And deep down, I know you believe what I am telling you."

The old woman's confidence in her story made a compelling argument. As she stood there, Angela couldn't help but buy into at least a small portion of what she was claiming.

You're pregnant. It wasn't like the thought hadn't crossed her mind while puking roadside. Impossible as the two words sounded to her ears, she knew they held some truth. She felt it. Inside her, grew life. *New* life. A child. *[we do not speak his name]*'s brother or sister.

The thought of having a baby, a new responsibility to look after, filled her chest with a familiar sense of comfort.

"I know this is all a lot to take in," Rosalyn said. "And I want to tell you more. I want you to know everything." She scooted her chair closer to Angela. At first, she seemed hesitant to reach out and place a calming hand on Angela's shoulder, but once it was there, she squeezed, a gentle way of letting her know she wouldn't have to face the maleficent spirit alone. "Let me run up to my room. I have books there. With incantations inscribed in them. They will help us. Together, we can battle this incubus. Send the daemon back to the Everywhere, for good this time. Where it belongs."

"And…"

"Your boy?"

Angela nodded.

"We will see. The Everywhere is a dark, nasty place. It's a place that exists between the living and the dead, a place that is and isn't. When a lost soul travels into the Everywhere, it's very hard to find its way back. The longer a soul resides in that dismal environment, the less chance it has of returning the same way it left. Once we locate the dream goblin—"

"Locate it?"

"Yes. We have to find it."

"And how do we do that?"

The old woman shrugged. "It could be anybody. We'll have to draw it out of hiding."

Angela shook her head. "Hold up. What do you mean it could *be* anybody? What are you saying? It's a person?"

"It very well could be. Someone you know or have met."

He's still alive, you know? The pharmacist's assistant. Not only had the pills she had given her messed with her birth control, but she had said those words with such… *knowledge.* Like she knew he was alive, and not figuratively. Angela recalled her wry smile as the words had left the girl's mouth.

"The girl in the pharmacy. She knew. She said exactly what you did. That he's alive. And my prescription. She gave me the wrong one. Abbie—Dr. Wilson—knew I was on birth control and how important *not* being pregnant was to me. She wouldn't have given me something to tamper with that."

"It could be, Mrs. Shepard. It could be the girl. These creatures usually enjoy influencing someone close to you. It could literally be anyone. But don't lose sight of who it *wants.*" Keeping her eyes trained on Angela, Rosalyn tilted her head down. "That person is you."

Again, she found herself doubting the words falling from the woman's lips, but she couldn't find the strength to argue. She needed more from her. She needed to see this thing through, however bat-shit-crazy her ideas sounded. "Okay, what do we do next?"

"Wait here a second. I'll go get my favorite grimoire."

Angela sat on the couch and waited for Rosalyn to return. For what seemed like a lifetime, she stared out the bay window, down the cul-de-sac, at her car. She found herself trapped in a daydream of nothing in particular, transfixed by the white cloud of blank thoughts before her. In that moment, she felt weightless. Untethered from gravity. Free from whatever fate that kept her grounded.

About thirty minutes later, she snapped out of her divine reverie. Her vision zoomed out, back into the dim lighting of Rosalyn Jeffries's living room. She checked her watch and realized how much time had passed. *Didn't she say she'd only be gone a minute?* Glancing up the stairs, she listened for movement, rustling from the old woman who seemed to still be digging through her massive collection of spells and books on the occult. Thirty minutes was a long time, massive collection or not.

"Rosalyn?" she called up the stairs.

Angela rose from the couch and padded over to the foot of the stairs. She peered up, staring into the still shadows above. "Rosalyn?" she asked the dark of the hallway, and for a second time she received no answer.

Oh Christ, she thought as she began her ascent. She wondered if she had been so trapped in her empty reveries that she had missed the woman walking back down the stairs. Maybe she had left to retrieve the necessary ingredients to ward off these supposed dream goblins. She hadn't remembered seeing the Oldsmobile in the driveway, and she debated whether to go back and check that first before going any farther. *Screw it,* she thought, making her way to the top of the stairs and staring down the hall.

"Rosalyn?" Reluctantly putting one foot forward, she eventually journeyed forth on weak, wobbly knees. "Rosalyn, can you hear me?"

The bedroom's French doors were already open, inviting her in.

As she stepped into the doorway, her stomach mixed what little contents remained, threatening another revolt. The smell hit her before she turned the corner, but by then it was too late; the decision to intrude had been made. At first, she thought it was only the chickens, but her sixth sense kicked in and told her differently, that the rancid odor was compounded by another, new stench.

Rosalyn's head had been set on the right side of the headboard, on the farthest golden-knobbed spike, hanging there like a baseball cap. Stripes of scarlet twisted and crisscrossed their way down to the bottom of the brass pole. Her grayish-brunette hair, which was now tainted with dark orange tones, had been mussed with hot wet blood. The rest of her body lay crumpled in the corner like some lazy teenager's soiled laundry. The murder weapon was staged on the bed, a fine-toothed saw taken from the garage, one of Rosalyn's husband's reliable tools she had never had the heart to toss out. The saw blade was covered in crimson, as was the comforter on which it rested. Little shredded scraps of flesh were wedged between the saw teeth. Angela backed into the hallway, her eyes jumping from the saw back to the woman's severed head, landing first on the ragged red outline of her dangling flesh. Then she lifted her gaze, stopping at Rosalyn's eyes; they weren't wide with bewilderment or abject horror as one might expect when looking malice in the face, knowing the grisly end was near—instead, her final expression was calm, almost peaceful, as if she knew exactly how she'd be handed her fate, accepting it honorably. Her mouth wasn't agape or shaped to indicate that she had cried out for help in her final seconds, but closed and tightlipped, as if she were keeping something inside from crawling out.

What secrets you had, my little Rosalyn, an unknown voice spoke deep from within Angela's subconscious.

Just then, a warm breeze flew in through the open window, brushing Angela's hair against her cheek. Whoever had savagely butchered the old woman had escaped through the window, dove out onto the roof, jumped down to the patio, and was halfway to the state border by now.

She glanced over at the phone stationed on the dresser. Next to the cradle, an orange light blinked, glowing and fading. She hustled over to the piece of ornate furniture, her first thought to call 911 and get them over here as quickly as possible. That time was of the essence when it came to catching murderers. The more she delayed the less chance they had of tracking down the bastard. Hot trails get awfully cold, awfully quickly, or so those true crime shows always said.

As she snatched up the phone, her thoughts swam. Too many ideas and opinions populated at once. For one thing, why had someone killed Rosalyn? It was too much of a coincidence to be a simple robbery. Besides, judging from the condition of the room, it didn't look like they had taken anything. Her jewelry box remained where it had been, next to the pile of dead chickens. No, this was an execution, plain and simple.

A deliberate act which raised many questions. Another thought: *why didn't they kill me too?* Whoever had committed the crime had to know the woman wasn't alone, that Angela was there, present within the house; her car wasn't exactly hidden being on the street corner. Furthermore, whatever secrets Rosalyn knew, she had relayed some of them to Angela. Did she not tell her enough? What else did the woman know? What was it that had gotten her killed?

Rosalyn, what else did you need to tell me?

The room spun as her brain fabricated endless possible answers. All at once, things suddenly became very real, very dark. Shadows crawled across the room, draping darkness over the walls, and Angela could feel them slipping inside her soul, poisoning her spirits, sullying her composure. The phone trembled in her hand and the fringes of her vision blurred.

The orange light winked: *1 NEW MESSAGE.*

Curiosity bested her, and she pressed play.

"This is 911 services, we received your call. We will be sending help—"

She didn't remember calling. Had she called? And forgotten about it? No, that seemed like a conversation she'd remember, though her mind had been so scattered lately she thought it was possible. She had called and forgotten in what? The span of five minutes? No, that didn't seem right. She checked the "placed calls" log and saw the three digit number had been dialed eight minutes ago, well before she'd crossed the bedroom's threshold.

Then it clicked.

Fuck.

She immediately rushed down the stairs, stampeding down them as if whoever had killed Rosalyn Jeffries was right behind her. She rushed across the foyer, ripped open the door, and expected to see the entire cul-de-sac packed with police vehicles and cops, special task force personnel with their weapons drawn and ready to fire on the old woman's murderer.

But there was no one. The street was as empty as it had been when she'd arrived. Birds whistled. Wind rustled the tree branches. Scattered leaves scuttled across the asphalt.

And, in the distance, she heard sirens, a consistent wail that always sounded farther than it actually was.

She doubled back for her purse, which she had left in the kitchen; made sure her pills were inside and bolted for the front door. Sprinting down the street, she fumbled around for her keys, locating them in the bottom of her bag. A long stream of curses spilled past her lips, and she continued scolding herself for being so stupid, for parking so far away. She knew she couldn't have predicted this outcome, but still, prepping for an emergency getaway would have been smart, something she would have thought about had her head not been clouded by recent events.

As the sirens grew louder, she reached the car. They still hadn't pulled into the cul-de-sac when she peeled out of there, searching the neighborhood windows for prying eyes. There were none that she could see, and she turned back to the road, focusing on her escape, putting weight on the gas pedal, pressing it to the floor.

Speeding down the highway, she passed several emergency response units heading in the opposite direction. None of them paid her any attention, yet she drove all the way back to Red River feeling like there was a bomb in place of her heart, ready to detonate at any moment.

VIII.

LOVE IS THE END OF ALL THINGS

The second she stepped foot inside her own home, she closed the door, clutched her aching chest, leaned against the door, slid to the floor, and began shaking with the onset of crippling sadness. The tears came fast, too quickly for her to prepare, and the heaving sobs attacked just as abruptly. Her whole body quaked as she purged the overflowing emotions inhibiting her to think clearly. After a few minutes of self-loathing and wondering where it had all gone wrong—where *she* had gone wrong—she glanced up. Through blurred vision, she made out her husband leaning against the door jamb between the foyer and the kitchen. He was watching her with his arms folded across his chest.

"I thought you were spending the night at your mom's?" he asked.

No *'Hey, babe! How are you? Is everything okay?'* The way he spoke made her feel like she'd done something wrong.

"I was. I was, but…"

"Are you all right?" he asked, his voice lacking concern. He acted like he couldn't see the evidence of her grief streaming down her face. "Everything okay?"

"No…" she said, shaking her head. "No, everything is most certainly not."

"What's wrong?"

To answer the question honestly would bring forth an admission of lies. She opted for the safe way out. "I just… couldn't sleep there. I wanted to be here. Home. With you."

"I thought this house was the reason you left." He sighed. "And... I thought maybe you were mad at me."

"I did want to get away from this house. This place is draining me dry, Terry. You have no idea." Using her sleeve, she brushed away a cheek's worth of tears. "But it doesn't matter. As long as I have you. You make it bearable."

He smiled genuinely. "Aw. Babe, come here." He strolled over to her, extending his arms. She took his hands and he yanked her to her feet. "Give me a hug."

She squeezed him tightly and things had never felt so good.

A shadow appeared in the kitchen doorway. "Hello, Angela."

She jumped out of her husband's arms, her heart hurtling. "What... what are you doing here?"

Before the figure in the doorway could answer, Terry put his hand on his wife's back and said, "Doctor Wilson dropped by. She figured we should talk. That my inclusion in your therapy might be healthy."

Abbie Wilson smiled and nodded. "I know in our therapy sessions you often mentioned how you wish Terry could join us, and how you were against approaching him."

Angela cleared her throat. "It's fine. He knows."

Abbie's smile widened. "I know. It's wonderful." She crossed the foyer and snatched her coat off the hook on the pantry door. "Well, I must be going. I have important plans tonight. I just wanted to drop by and introduce myself to Terry, try to convince him. Looks like I didn't need to." She made her way to the door. "Goodnight, you two. I'll have my secretary schedule our first couple's session."

After she left, Terry said, "She seems nice."

"Yeah, real nice."

"What's the matter? I thought this is what you wanted?"

"I did. *I do.* I just..."

"What?"

"I feel weird."

"Weird how?"

She closed her eyes, trying to find a way to describe her emotions without coming off clinically insane. "Weird in a lot of ways, I guess. Dr. Wilson was the last person I expected to come home and see. Plus, I've had a strange night."

"Hallucinations?"

[Rosalyn's head on a pike, blood pouring down the brass stake in thin runnels.] Not a hallucination.

"No, they've been quiet."

"Good. Glad to hear. How have you been feeling otherwise?"

"Good. I guess. I'm not sure. Exactly how do you mean?"

"I don't know. Just asking. Being a concerned husband, that's all," he said, almost defensively.

In truth, he sounded concerned. Overly concerned now, the opposite of how he had acted when she'd first come home. Angela didn't think much of it, but there was a small part of her that thought he knew where she had been. It was like he could smell the great outdoors on her flesh, Rosalyn Jeffries's blood in her hair. She pushed those thoughts far, far away, burying them in the back of her mind. Right now, all she wanted was her pillow and eight hours of uninterrupted sleep.

"Okay, I'm going to shower and hit the hay. That okay?"

"Yeah, sure. There's leftover turkey and gravy in the fridge if you want some."

[Rosalyn's calm gaze. Her close-lipped expression. The bloody saw on the bed. Bits of her shredded flesh wedged between the metal teeth.]

"No, I don't have much of an appetite."

"Okay," he said, smooching her forehead. "Let me finish up down here and I'll meet you in bed."

As she soaked in the tub, she wondered who had killed Rosalyn Jeffries, and more importantly—why. It didn't add up. The woman had done nothing, absolutely nothing that warranted her execution, and now there she was, her head topping the headboard like the last loser of some violent Viking siege. Who would want her dead? Who could do this?

She kept waiting for a phone call from the police or a knock on the front door from two detectives wanting to question her on the woman's brutal demise. Or Barry. *Fuck,* she thought, closing her eyes, holding her breath, and slipping under the water. She recalled telling Barry that the old woman was following her. If the police did question anyone, surely they'd talk to Barry. He would tell them what Angela had said over the phone.

She couldn't remember if she had told him her intentions, that she was on the way to the woman's house as they spoke. If she had, that'd make her an easy target. Suspect number one, without a doubt. Hell, it might even be enough to arrest her. She didn't know how much evidence it would take to incriminate her, but with her recent struggles—all of them well documented on *Let's Switch Houses!*—bringing her in and pinning the murder on her would be a no-brainer, especially if they could verify she was in the house that afternoon. And she figured they could. All it would take was one fingerprint or a nosey neighbor to identify her car. Hell, they could check her E-Z Pass and see her path of travel.

Yep, she was fucked on all counts.

Fuck, fuck, fuck.

It was after midnight and she couldn't believe they hadn't come for her yet.

She figured she'd enjoy one last bath before being hauled off to jail and earning a life sentence.

When she came up for air and opened her eyes, she was startled by the figure sitting on the toilet, staring directly at her.

She screamed.

The figure didn't budge.

"Holy shit," she said, leaning her head gently against the tiled shower enclosure. "You nearly made me pee."

"Sorry," Terry said, leaning against the reservoir tank. He didn't sound like he was all-too sorry. Much like earlier, he didn't seem concerned at all.

"Terry," she said, closing her eyes. "I was hoping to have a little privacy."

"Sorry, babe. But I think we need to talk."

Oh shit! They're here! The cops!

"Christ, Terry, what is it? What's so important you can't wait ten minutes?"

"I know where you went today," he said calmly.

Her heart slammed to a stop. "W-what?"

"I know *exactly* where you went today," he said, a grin halving his face. Before she could find the words, her husband removed a sharp, serrated blade speckled with brown stains. "And I know you saw what I did."

IX.

I DID IT ALL IN THE NAME OF LOVE AND FORGIVENESS

Honey," she said, the two syllables coming out in very different pitches. "Terry, you're scaring me."

His grin didn't falter. As he began to respond, his eyes fell to the knife in his hand. "You know, I was really hoping the cops would get there quicker," he said, his smile diminishing. "What is it with those pricks? Don't they understand what a goddamn emergency is?"

"Terry…"

He pressed a finger against his lips, hushing her. "Don't make this harder, babe. Please don't. God, this would have been so much easier if they had just hauled you off to jail. You would have been safe there."

She felt her teeth clacking together, chattering from the chill running over her bones. "Safe from what?"

He looked at her with crooked eyes, as if she should already know. "Well, from yourself, of course. You're not well, Angie. Hallucinations. Crazy ideas. Imagining things taking place between our walls. An old woman dancing naked in our living room. That's crazy stuff, babe. Just plain crazy." He swallowed. "You have to take care of yourself now that you're going to be a mother again."

The words came out like a shotgun blast from point-blank range. "How… how the hell do you know that?"

"She told me."

Her jaw dropped, hung open while she tried to fit the pieces together. "Rosalyn? Rosalyn told you?"

His brow arched. "No, the *other* woman."

"What other woman?" Tears streamed down her face. "Terry, you're not making sense."

"Ester Moore," Terry said. "The woman Barry told you about. The one who was part of the coven with Rosalyn Jeffries back in the 60s."

Pure confusion trapped her face. "How…"

Terry waved his hand in the air nonchalantly. "Barry called me earlier. Said he thought he'd worked you into a panic by telling you about Rosalyn's past. But there's no need to panic, babe. I'm here to help you. Here to help see you through these next difficult steps."

"Don't call me, babe."

Terry reacted as if she'd backhanded him across the face. "Please, don't act like—"

"You killed her. You killed Rosalyn Jeffries."

"I had to. Don't you understand? She was feeding you lies. She was trying to tear apart our family. Don't you get it? She set us up! She was responsible for us going on *Switch!* Ester Moore wants to help us. She wants to help us get our son back. Isn't that great?" The excitement in his voice brought shivers down her spine, perpetual coldness to her muscles. Her husband sounded manic, a prime candidate for the psychiatric hospital where Dr. Wilson had mentioned she should voluntarily commit herself. "Ester wants to help us get our son back from the Everywhere, where the dream goblin is keeping him. It's a nasty thing that dream goblin, so Ester says. The damned thing attached itself to this house. It wants you, Angela. It wants to *become* you."

"Terry…"

"But Ester says she can stop it. Give it what it wants." His face turned still as stone. "A *replacement.*" His eyes drifted to her belly. "The… *child* growing inside you."

"Terry, I can't be pregnant."

"Yes, you can. I've seen it. In my dreams."

"Terry, we had sex three nights ago. It's too early to tell."

"It came to me in a dream," he spoke, his jaw clenched. "I saw it. You're pregnant."

She recalled what Rosalyn had said and the warning label on the prescription. In truth, she felt pregnant, *very pregnant*, and, if she stayed still long enough, she swore she felt something swimming inside her, an unnatural flutter of some ungodly new life growing exponentially.

"Okay, Terry. Suppose I am. What then?"

"You carry it to term. You hand it over to Ester Moore. She retrieves our precious child from the Everywhere and gives him back. It's a switch. Straight up." His eyes leaked, slowly emitting tears. "This is the switch we need, baby. *This is the switch we need.*"

Her lips trembled. "I'm not pregnant, Terry. Please get that through your head. Right fucking now."

He offered a phony smile; the one Terry usually displayed when he was pissed and not doing a great job of hiding it. "You're right. Maybe I'm getting a little carried away." He stood up and reached under the sink, grabbing the small box of home pregnancy tests. Turning to her, he held out the box, offering her the pick of the lot as if they were something desirable like lollipops. "Pee on one of these bad boys. Prove me right."

"Terry, it's too early, it won't—"

He dropped the box on the floor, marched over to the tub, and gripped her by her hair. With one tug, he lifted her from her seat. Mindful that he could rip out a huge patch of her hair with little effort, she went with the momentum and hurled herself over the side, landing with her back on the tile. He yanked her to her knees, and, on all fours, she faced the scattered box of tests.

"You will piss on one of these," he said, spittle spraying from his lips. His shadow sprawled over her and his breath brushed against her ear. "Or I swear to God, I will carve *his* name into your chest, setting a daily reminder of all that pain, all that guilt you can so easily throw away. Got it?"

"You're insane," she said in a tone barely above a breath.

"Say his name," he demanded. "You vowed to never speak it again, but I want to hear you say it."

"No." Teardrops puddled on the tile before her, three at a time. "No, I will not."

Her head suddenly jerked back. She felt hot pain on her neck, above her larynx. Scarlet droplets materialized before her, mixing with the fallen tears.

"You will say his name or I will open your throat right here and now." Terry growled in her ear. She couldn't believe how unhinged he'd become. Was he always like this? Capable of such psychotic actions? Or was this a slow-building end? Had Terry been slowly falling apart? Did she miss the warning signs because she was too wrapped up in her own shit? No, she didn't think so. The man she married, the man she'd spent the last few days trying to help right the ship steering their marriage was very different from the man standing over her, threatening to end her life.

These creatures usually enjoy influencing someone close to you, the old woman had said.

"You're not my husband," she said, pinching her eyes shut. "You're not Terry."

"No?" He bit her ear, hard enough to leave behind deep, toothy pockets, but lacking the power to break the skin. "Who am I?"

"You're the dream goblin."

With this, Terry reared his head back and laughed. "You are something else, Angie. That woman got you all mixed up, didn't she? Rosalyn. She turned us against each other, baby. She's convinced you I'm evil. Well, I'm not evil. She was. I'm glad I killed her. Ester told me I had to, had to get her out of our way so we can proceed with the plan. *The switch."* A soft, demonic giggle rose in Terry's throat. "Rosalyn tried to interfere and she got what she deserved. Lesson learned. DO NOT INTERFERE."

"You're fucking nuts!"

A sharp pain shot through her neck, and, in that moment, she thought he'd begun sawing his way through her esophagus, working the blade deep into her vertebrae. She expected to see geysers of blood spurt forth, slicking the tile floor with scarlet, but no such image came forth. The pain was either a product of faulty nerves or her imagination conspiring against her. Seconds later, the pain ebbed and eventually faded. The red droplets had slowed to a stop.

"Dream goblins," Terry said, chuckling. "We'll teach 'em. Ester will show us the way."

"Who... is... Ester?"

Terry squealed with delight. In a whisper, he told her, "Do not ask questions to which you already know the answer."

Too tired to hold her position, Angela felt her arms give. She lowered herself onto the floor, laying flat, pressing her cheek against the cool tile. "Terry... don't hurt me."

"I am your husband. Your dearest, forgiving husband who has been patient with you, who has waited a long time for you to right all the wrong you caused our family. Who has been patiently waiting for you to snap out of it. God... you don't know how hard it's been on me. Every day I think about leaving you, Angela. Every *goddamn* day." She was surprised to hear him sounding like her husband again, nothing manic about his voice whatsoever. Surprised... and terrified of what was coming out of his mouth. *The truth,* she thought. "I always thought that would be an easy way out. Just leave and I'll never have to see *him* in your stupid fucking face again. My little *[we do not speak his name]*, here and present, living through the image of his psychotic fucking mother."

She said something, but the words barely made it past her lips.

"What was that?" He relieved some of the pressure his knee applied to her back.

"I said..." She coughed, a deep honking noise, goose-like. She lifted her head a few inches from the floor. "I said... we promised to never speak his name. The both of us."

She felt something pound her in the back of the head. Her face smashed against the tile. It took her several seconds to realize he had driven his fist into the back of her skull. A second after, her head launched backward, her neck stretching to its peak flexibility. Cold metal pressed against her neck again, and she wondered if her bones would break before he seized the opportunity to split open her jugular.

"I want you to say it for me, baby," he rasped in her ear, the demonic version of her husband returning. "I want you to speak his goddamn name. It's been so long since you've said it. It'll feel good, I promise. Like a weight lifting off your shoulders. Or, in this case, a knife leaving the most vulnerable part of your body."

"*No,*" she croaked.

"Yes." He snarled in her ear, a cruel noise that sent shivers slithering down her spine. "Yes, you goddamn will."

"NO."

"YES." He pulled her head back farther, cracking something in her throat.

"*NO!*" she screamed as loud as her strained voice permitted.

He slammed her head forward, crunching her nose against the tiled floor. A Rorschach pattern of blood appeared under her face. He pulled back her head again, slowly, allowing her to take in the scarlet sights before her. Crimson flowed down her face, steadily as a mountain brook.

"Say it, you bitch, or I swear to God I'm slitting your shit open right here and now!"

She opened her mouth, fully expecting to comply with her husband's demands, but the only thing that came out was an inarticulate fragment of a word followed by a bout of heaving sobs. She tried again but ended up howling for help, screaming the neighbor's name. This earned her another meet-and-greet with the floor, and she heard the violence of her nose shattering over the impact.

"Last chance," he said. "Last chance to make this right, Angela. I'm a forgiving husband. Very loving. I can forgive a lot. I can forgive you for all your mistakes, your transgressions against our family. I can forgive you for losing our son, our only-fucking-child, the one thing in life that mattered above all else." The man applying intense pressure to her throat wept. *Maybe,* she thought, *maybe he's still a man after all.* "I'm a loving and forgiving husband, Angela," he repeated, his voice cracking through the sobs. "I want you to make this right. I'm not asking for much."

She had no idea what to say. Anything, she thought, was apt to get her killed.

Keeping quiet, she listened to one last demand.

"Say. His. Fucking. Name."

He wasn't crying anymore, and his voice had a ring of finality to it, like there wouldn't be another request, and certainly no more opportunities to resolve this mess.

Speak his name or die.

Those were her choices.

She opened her mouth, and something like a breath fell out.

Terry sobbed again. Loud, as if something in his chest had suddenly fractured.

"I'm sorry," he whispered into her ear.

She felt the blade split her flesh, sink in. A warm splash coated her throat.

"WILLIAM!" The name exploded from her mouth, with it, a gob of saliva and blood. "His name was *William.*" As her husband removed the weapon from her throat, she wailed with relief, frustration, and crushing sadness. She laid her forehead in the small pool of blood and saliva. Body violently trembling, she crawled away from her attacker, toward the door.

"Nuh-uh, Angela," Terry said from behind her. He gripped her ankle. She was too weak to resist. "We're not done yet." As he bent down to retrieve a test, he wiped the glistening tears off his cheeks. "I hope you still have some urine left in that body of yours."

X.

POSITIVE AND NEGATIVES

Sure enough, Terry was right—she was pregnant. Or so the stick she pissed on told her. It wasn't one of those cheap sticks either—it was one of those early detection pieces. And even so, she still believed her eyes were unveiling lies; no at-home pregnancy kit on the planet would test positive this early, not three days after the deal was sealed. Quick math told her it should be at least another week and a half before the test would display positive results—alas, here it was. The plus sign glared up at her like the eye of some dead cartoon character. The realization kicked her brain into the endless possibilities of how this was possible, each stray thought reverting back to notions of dream goblins and dream worlds and things that just didn't exist. Still, she stared down at a bona fide miracle.

In other words, an *immaculate conception.*

This has to be a dream, she thought, *another hallucination.*

Terry paced the room. "I knew it. I fucking knew it!"

Slowly, Angela shook her head. "This isn't possible."

"Yes," he said, getting down on his knees before her. She wasn't sure if he was re-proposing or getting in prime position to wedge the blade between her ribs. "Yes, it is."

Just looking at him made the small, shallow furrow on her throat burn. "How? How am I pregnant? Besides the other night, we haven't fucked in over nine months. I haven't slept with anyone…"

"…since William?" he asked.

She nodded.

"You still won't say his name?" The disappointment in his voice was disconcerting.

She swallowed her own spit and that hurt, too. "Not unless you're going to threaten me again."

He shook his head like a wet pup. "I'm sorry, babe. I'm so goddamn sorry." He placed a hand on her knee. It felt cold, impossibly frigid, like an icicle come summertime. There was something wild in his eye, something telling her the stress of everything was too much and Terry had finally snapped. Maybe this Ester Moore, whoever she was, knew how to push his buttons, knew how to make him cross the line of no turning back. Every psychologist on the planet would rule him utterly insane on his appearance alone, one look in those feral eyes. "But you had to say it. You had to let it out. You had to speak his name. *William. William* likes when you speak his name." He glanced down at her stomach.

She followed his peculiar gaze. "What are you talking about?"

He pointed at her stomach with the knife. She recoiled.

"That's our Will in there," he said confidently, the words bringing an endearing smile to his face.

"What the fucking shit are you talking about?" Angela asked, and something behind her eyes began to burn. She thought it might be her brain melting from the insanity. *He actually believes this.* She hadn't forgotten how he'd admitted to killing Rosalyn Jeffries and came very close to opening her throat like a sandwich bag, spilling its contents across the bathroom floor.

"Not our Will, not exactly. But a copy. The dream goblin wants the real William, but it'll settle for a copy, an imitation. Ester says so. She can make a trade. *The switch.*"

As if she hadn't known ten minutes ago, she now understood this was no longer the man she'd married, the man she had fallen in love with once upon a time ago, the man she'd wanted to have babies with, lots and lots of babies. Nor was he the man she wanted to grow old with, have their ashes combined and scattered across their favorite Jersey Shore beaches. This was another man. A man who had, like a fine piece of fruit, grown rotten and sick, decayed from the inside out. She knew it was partially her fault—if she had been more responsible and been watching their son a little more closely that day, then none of this would be happening. In fact, if the tragic event hadn't transpired, the three of them would probably be on the couch right about now, eating bowls of homemade ice cream sundaes and watching *LEGO BATMAN* on Blu-ray.

This is all your fault, she thought. *You deserve this.*

"Terry…" she said, tears streaming out of her eyes. "…you're sick."

He only smiled at this. "No, baby. I've never felt better. This is how we get on. This is how we get through. Fuck therapy, fuck house-swaps, fuck moving and selling. This—" he placed his hand on her bloated stomach, "This is how we heal."

"Terry, I love you. I really do. But this is so wrong. Everything about this feels so wrong."

He placed his hands between her thighs, knife included, resting all three on the edge of the toilet bowl. She looked down at the tip of the blade. If he wanted, one upward motion would plunge the knife into the softest flesh under her chin.

"I dreamt this," he said. "I dreamt you were pregnant again, with our Will. That we were able to reincarnate him. Give him new life so we can gain back the old one."

A blurry smear filled her vision. "Terry, I don't care what this test shows, I'm not pregnant. This is a trick. Whatever it is, it's a trick. Your dreams, Terry, they lied to you."

He scowled. "Dreams don't lie. Not in this house. Don't you see that?"

Blanching, she glared at him. "You've seen the hallucinations, too?"

Terry's face twisted into wrinkles, lines creasing his face like a brown paper bag. In a brief fit of rage, he buried the knife in the plasterboard over Angela's wild, knotted hair. White dust sprinkled the top of her cowering head.

"I am not hallucinating!" he yelled as he stomped his foot on the tile, making the entire room vibrate. He marched over to the far wall where Angela had put a piece of duct tape over the hole that had once shown her things existing in faraway worlds. "Look through there," he demanded, ripping the tape away. A small beam of light filtered through. "Look in there and tell me what you see."

Crying, she shook her head. "No."

"Do it." He bared his teeth like some savage beast born in the wild and raised on a steady diet of violence. "Goddammit, do it, or I swear to

Christ I will rip our unborn son from your womb and make you fucking eat him."

The look in his eyes suggested he might actually do that, or something equally vile. She removed herself from her position on the toilet and crawled on all fours toward the small pinprick of light. Once in the path of the beam, she felt a warmth infiltrate her bones, and not in the comforting way the morning sun sometimes felt on the back of her neck, how it sometimes soaked into her skin. This was a dark warmth, a conquering warmth. It made her feel like maggots were hosting a party beneath her flesh, an all-encompassing death orgy.

When close, Terry reached out and grabbed her by her hair, guiding her toward the hole. With force, her eye met the opening and she peered through, her body teeming with the sick shine the aperture emitted.

[*It's the house, but it isn't their house. It sits in the middle of the Everywhere, the surrounding world a blanket of dirt, a boneyard of old souls, lost and wandering, eternally trapped here. She pushes her way past the spirits, their amoebic shapes swirling in the atmosphere, disappearing when touched. Before blinking out of existence, their physical manifestations disperse like dandelion seeds, wafting into the air, floating over her head, swallowed up by the sheet of darkness reigning above.*

She moves toward the house, paying the souls no mind. They speak to her in different tongues, some of them coherent, most of them not. She ignores the warbling of their combined voices and pushes forward, up the steps and onto the porch. The front door stands ajar and little effort is required to swing it open, as if someone opens it simultaneously with her touch. She steps into the living room, her eyes immediately glancing down at the vase stuffed with old, wilted flowers, blackened petals matching the cold, dead sky above. She makes her way across the carpet, toward the kitchen.

A shadow waits for her.

A hip-high shadow with no face, and a name she has so desperately tried to forget, forced out of her memory. But the name sticks. And she knows it well.

Ma-me, the faceless shadow says in that familiar tone. Ma-me, home.

Tears leave her eyes, roll down her face. Music plays from somewhere in the distance, something harmonic and keyed, something ambient. It's like a movie score, she thinks, the soundtrack of her life and death.

Ma-me, the shadow speaks, stepping into the light. Ma-me. Where-go?

She musters enough courage to tell the shadow she hasn't gone anywhere; that she's right here, and God, she's not leaving. Not ever. Not again.

Ma-me. Where-put-me?

Invisible hands wring her heart. She can almost hear her essential organ breaking in her chest.

Ma-me, love-me?

The boy steps into the living-room light.

It's not the same boy she remembers. His skin is dirty, mottled with patches of missing flesh. Maggots squirm in the craters of his carved muscle, teeming out of the wounds, falling onto the floor by the handfuls. He's missing one eye, and the other is covered in a film of milky white. Deep lacerations have been cut into his face, trenches of glistening red. His hair is caked with dirt, disheveled, mussed with mud and other earthly sediments. The clothes he'd been wearing on the day he left are torn and ragged, soiled beyond distinction, but still, she knows they are the same clothes.

She knows.]

"Oh my God," she whispered.

"Is it him?" Terry asked. "Is it my boy?"

"William…"

[I thought you loved me, Ma-me.

I do, son, I do. She says this over and over again, her reassuring mantra.

Follow me, the boy-who-is-not-William says.

He walks backward until the darkness of the kitchen wraps its shadows around him, concealing his grotesque figure. Something pushes her ahead; one foot follows the other, and, before she knows it, she's in the kitchen, looking out the back door. Outside, the-boy-who-is-not-William hops off the bottom stair, his feet landing in the wet dirt. She follows him out the door, down the stairs, planting her feet on the surface, allowing her toes to sink into the overturned earth. A chill rises up her legs, corkscrewing her bones. Her flesh hardens, breaking out in raised bumps as the fear settles in the base of her spine, propelling her along at the daydream's command. The boy points to the shed in the corner of the yard; beyond it lays a wasteland of dug-up earth and scattered human bones.

The left shed door sits slightly ajar. She catches a glimpse of something moving in the space between the doors, slithering like a snake in midnight shadows. She realizes it's a hand. Dark green flesh mottled with black spots, reptilian-like smoothness. The night's natural lighting—which is minimal—gleams off its cold skin. Curled fingers topped with hooked nails, perfect for slicing and dicing the fleshy surface of its enemies. A single finger rises from the rest, waves, beckons her, and invites her inside.

Distance has killed the background music, and now, there is utter silence. She drifts across the dirt and steps over half-buried bones, beginning the short, soundless trek toward the dream goblin's domain.]

Outside now. She'd led him out the back door, across the dirt lot that made up the backyard.

A breeze broke across her face. Moonlight flooded her vision. She concentrated on the shed, her eyes straining against the visible dark.

"The shed," a voice whispered in her ear. "The shed."

"That's where I last saw him."

"That's what you told them," Terry said, his words whistling through clenched teeth. "That's what you told the cops, the detectives, and the district attorney."

"He went back there to play, and…"

"…and?"

"He never came back."

Terry grabbed her, spun her, and shook her violently.

"I don't believe you!" he hissed.

["Ma-me?" asks the boy who is very much William.

Sunlight now fills the yard. It's warm and comforting and the feeling sinks all the way down into her toes. Looking up at the bright afternoon sky, Angela smiles.

"Ma-me?" William asks as he squeezes her hand.

"Yes, baby?"

"Ma-me." That's all he says. That's all he'll ever say, so the doctors tell her. "Ma-me?" Terry doesn't think so. He says the doctors don't know squat—after all, they're not fortune-tellers. The boy who is William can snap out of it at any moment or, hell—grow out of it. Doctors don't know everything.

She doesn't share the same notions.

She closes her eyes, allowing the sunlight to bathe her before she slips into the darkness the shed provides. "Do you want to play a game?"

"Ma-me."

She opens the shed door. With a hand on William's back, she guides him inside. "Come on, honey. Let's play a game."

"Ma-me."

They walk inside. The shed stands completely empty. Since the house has two garages, there is no need for the extra space.

She closes the door behind them, shutting out the light. The only brightness in the room comes from the lone window opposite the wall from where they had entered. Everywhere else is dark and painted with shadows. "Close your eyes, pumpkin."

William does as he's told. Such a good little boy, obedient. Always does as he's told.

She takes the kitchen knife she's been lugging around all day, the same weapon that would later be wielded by her husband, the same one that nearly ends her life.

"Keep your eyes closed, baby." She's crying now. In her mind, music plays. A sad song. Like the end of a sad movie when the credits are rolling. "Keep your eyes closed for mommy."

Like the good boy he is, William does as he's told.

"Ma-me," he says.

And she brings down the knife.]

"The cops found this knife," Terry whispered into her ear. "They found the weapon."

"No DNA," she said, her voice projecting into the darkness coating the shed's interior. An endless voice responded with still silence. "No DNA, and no body."

"Where did you put him?" Terry asked, putting the knife back to her throat. She felt the chalky dust of the sheetrock on her skin. "Please tell me, Angela," Terry cried. "For the love of God and all that is holy, please tell me what you did with our son, William. Did you give it to them? Did you give it those monsters?"

"He's safe," she whispered. "He's in a safe, safe place."

[The knife comes down, the metal blade sinking inches into the wooden floorboards. She backs the knife out of the uncovered subfloor and screams with frustration. The noise is loud and bestial, unsettling to human ears. She barely recognizes the sound as her own and she briefly wonders if it was, or if there was something else in the shed with her besides her damaged son.

William only stares blankly at his mother and asks, "Ma-me?"]

"He's in the Everywhere," Angela said, turning to her husband, no longer concerned with the knife at her throat. "This whole time we worried that our William is dead. But he's not. He's safe. He's alive, Terry, and he's safe!"

She recalled the pharmacist and her infinite words of wisdom: *"He's still alive,"* she had said, and wondered if the dream goblin had touched the woman from beyond, briefly hijacked her subconscious. In any case, the girl was right.

William was alive.

Somewhere.

[A crowded mall during peak shopping hours. A galley of benches. Angela sits down next to a couple who seems around the same age as she. She stations William between them.

"Thank you for showing up," the woman says, speaking in a low tone and refusing to glance in her direction. Both strangers sport dark sunglasses. The man has a baseball cap pulled down, the brim shielding the upper half of his face.

The mall is alive with shoppers and their passing conversations are enough to drown out their own.

"No problem," Angela says, her voice unsteady. She tries to keep her cool. She tries not to lose her shit. Terry has already grown suspicious, she's certain of it. He's noticed her odd behavior over the last week. He's been busy with work, so they haven't had time to "talk", but she knows he'll ask. The what's-wrong-with-you-nothing-honey conversation is inevitable. "Can we make this quick?"

"Ma-me," William says.

"He looks precious," the woman says.

"He's perfect," the man concurs.

Angela feels her stomach flip, her insides liquefying. Everything feels like jelly.]

"He's alive," Angela said, almost as if she were pleading. "Terry, he's alive and safe."

"No, Angela," her husband said, dropping the knife to his side. "No, he's gone. And you killed him. You killed him when you lost him. When you gave up on him."

Angela's face contorted. "I did not kill my son. I did not. Do you hear me? I DID NOT KILL HIM."

[Angela kisses her good boy on the top of his head.

With no discernible expression, he looks up at her and says, "Ma-me."

"May we ask what happened?" the man asks, pointing to his head. "Mentally, I mean."

Angela keeps her lips pressed against his scalp. She looks at the man, shooting him a sharp glance. "Just born that way. That's what they told me."

The woman doesn't act concerned. "He's perfect. Our client will be happy."

"Client. William won't be… in any danger, will he?"

The strangers shake their heads. The man speaks up first. "No, nothing like that. Our client is a very wealthy woman who enjoys helping those less fortunate. Those with certain mental abilities… they interest her."

"Abilities?" Angela asks, almost laughing. "You mean deficiencies?"

Neither stranger answers.

Angela lets the comment go, hoping the conversation will swing in another direction, toward the end. She doesn't enjoy the intense panic building in her chest, the numbness in her entire body. She'll consider herself lucky if she walks away from this thing without having a heart attack.

"I have to ask," Angela says, changing the subject. "How will you do it? Legally, I mean."

The woman answers promptly: "We have birth certificates, social security cards—we even have pictures of your son with our client, from birth on. Photoshopped. Very professional. Very credible. No one will question it. Trust me."

"This isn't our first rodeo," the man says, and there is something about his confidence that causes Angela's bones to shake.

"Are you ready to do this?" the woman asks.

"I think so," Angela answers, and she can't believe those words fly from her mouth so quickly.

"Did you destroy your hard drive?"

Angela nods. "Local computer nerd assured me our conversations will never see the light of day. I had to tell him I was cheating on my husband. I paid him in cash."

"Good." The man rubs the top of William's head. "Such a good boy."

"Don't seek us out," the woman adds. "If you try to find us or locate William, they will kill you."

Kill me?

"Excuse me?" Angela asks.

The man cracks a nervous smile. "That won't be necessary, Sharon," he says, then turns to Angela. "Right?"

"Right," she squeaks in response.

Who are these people?

"I have to ask… you know… for my own knowledge… but why? Why William? There are plenty of kids in the system? Why did you seek out my boy?"

The strangers look at each other, then shrug as if to say, no-harm-in-telling-you.

"Our client has her reasons," the woman says. "She's kept an eye on William for quite some time now."

"He's a very special boy."

But how? she wanted to ask but couldn't locate the courage to further the odd, unsettling conversation.

"I'm afraid we can't elaborate beyond that," the woman adds.

"I was just curious."

"Well, don't be," she says, her attitude changing, her voice cold and harsh. "You know about curiosity—it kills cats."

"I DID NOT KILL HIM."

There was a terrible look in her eyes. Terry glared at her with an equally murderous gaze.

She breathed hard. Her chest heaved in rapid succession.

Terry gritted his teeth, the muscles in his neck becoming visible cords. The knife fell from his hand and landed on the ground. "What did you do with him? Who took him from you? No one disappears, Angela. Fuck this dream goblin bullshit! You did something with him! I know it!"

[*She begins to sob*]

"I put him in a safe place," she said, her face glistening in the moonlight.

[*"You'll keep him safe?"*]

"Why?" Terry asked, the knife falling to the turned soil. He put his hands on the side of his head. "Why did you do anything with him? He was our son!" She'd never seen her husband cry so much before. As he wept, his entire body shuddered with the rhythm of his outbursts.

[*"He's safe with her. Where he's going, he'll have lots of friends to keep him company. The other boys and girls, special like him."*]

"I couldn't do it, Terry. I couldn't look at him anymore. I just couldn't. I know that makes me a horrible a person, but I couldn't do it."

"You bitch," he spat. "You bitch! YOU KILLED OUR SON!"

The blade near her feet reflected moonlight, catching her eye.

"I told you, I didn't kill him."

Quicker than Terry could react, she went for the knife.

[*They each take one of William's hands and begin walking, toward the hustling throng of shoppers.*

William glances back over his shoulder. Their eyes connect for one final moment.

"Ma-me," he says.

She closes her eyes as a wave of dysphoria bowls her over.

"Ma-me?"

When she opens them, the trio is farther, about to be swallowed up amongst the bustling pedestrians. She focuses on William's face, and she briefly thinks his face is filled with worry, which isn't possible because William doesn't worry, never has. He doesn't laugh or smile, frown or get angry. He doesn't do much at all. He's just...

...he's just William.

That's all he'll ever be.

She begins working on her lies, training herself to believe them.]

Terry bolted forward, grabbed for the knife, but he was too late. She snatched it first, and he immediately altered his intentions. Instead of scrambling on the floor for the only weapon, he barreled into his wife and knocked her back, sending her inside the shed.

The interior was utterly dark, the only light filtering in through the open door and the small awning window opposite the entryway. She wore the darkness like a cocoon, immediately crouching on her toes and creeping over to the darkest corner.

A shadow filled the entryway.

"Angela… why? Why did you do this to us? Why? Why? WHY?"

No more questions, she decided.

As he stepped foot inside the shed, she rushed forward, jamming the knife into where she thought her husband's neck was. A wet sucking sound interrupted the silence, leaving her ears as quickly as it had arrived. A sticky warmth flowed over her fingers, down her hands, tickling the nerves of her soft skin. With force, she withdrew the blade, and this time the wetness dotted her face.

Terry stumbled into the puddle of moonlight in the center of the shed with both hands wrapped around his neck, gushes of crimson squirting through the cracks of his fingers.

"I told you…" she said through her teeth, "I didn't kill our son. He's still alive. He is safe. He is with *her* in the Everywhere, you dumb fucking bastard!" She stabbed him again, this time in the back, between the shoulder blades. "YOU NEVER LISTENED TO ME!" She slipped the knife inside him again, this time in the ribcage, retracting it, stabbing, retracting it, stabbing, repeating the process over and over; flowers of scarlet blooming across his midsection. "YOU NEVER PAID ATTENTION! YOU WERE NEVER THERE FOR ME!" The next swipe slashed up his arm, ripping open fabric and flesh, creating a dark red furrow which spat copious amounts of blood. She drove the blade up under his arm, penetrating the soft muscle of his armpit. The blade stopped when it struck bone. "You never understood how I felt," she said, more calmly now. "About William. About our situation." She ripped the knife free and pointed it behind her, back toward the house. Scarlet dripped steadily off the tip. "About this house. I hate this fucking house. I never wanted to move here and you NEVER FUCKING LISTENED TO ME!"

Terry dropped to his hands and knees, coughing up a wad of dark—almost black—fluids. It spattered the floor before him. He tried to speak, but a mouthful of thick blood prevented the words from making it past his lips.

Angela kicked him in the ribs, where the knife had punched through flesh and cartilage, and flipped him over, onto his back. At the ceiling, he stared, his eyes starting to glaze over.

"You were never a good husband to me." She brought the knife to her side and stepped over him, placing a foot on each side of his body. She dropped to her knees, planting her bottom on his punctured midsection. "And an even worse father. Where were you during his doctor's appointments?"

He spat out a word that sounded like *working,* but it came out wet and unintelligible.

"Where were you during the countless hours of therapy?"

This time Terry kept quiet.

"Where were you, Terry? You were supposed to be there for me. *For us.*"

He grunted a word that might have been *sorry,* but a burst of scarlet sputtering over his lips was the only thing she could make out for certain.

"You were never there. Never there for me, never there for our boy. You abandoned us."

He didn't deny her account.

"Then you made us go on that stupid fucking show. For what? To repair us? To fix us? Our marriage isn't one of your stupid cars. You can't just turn a wrench and expect us to be okay, fine-fucking-dandy." She closed her eyes, breathed, and inhaled the metallic odor overruling the air. "There's no fixing us Terry. There's no fixing me. I'm the one who's damaged. I am the one who's broken... I'm... I'm..."

Angela raised the knife over her head and, without giving it much thought, buried the blade in the base of her husband's neck. Terry spasmed many times over the next sixty seconds—spastically at first, then intermittently—and then his body went stiff as a log, his flesh taking on frigid temperatures.

She sat on top of him for what seemed like the length of a long dream, ignoring the burn in her quads and staring through the awning window, at the moon, and wondering what lay beyond the stars. She imagined a sea with a pirate ship getting dragged beneath the black surface by massive tentacles. A house in the middle of some cosmic existence called the Everywhere. The skulking shadow of a boy she used to know. An endless, blue-lit room with wandering souls, most of them grotesque and previously savaged.

Before she could shove the blade in her own neck, ending her pathetic excuse of an existence, the night was filled with a cacophony of sirens and anxious voices. Just when the suicidal thoughts occurred and started to make sense, she felt hands grabbing her wrists and loud, commanding voices screaming in her ear. She resisted as much as she could, but all her energy had been spent on butchering her husband, and she was easily overpowered. It wasn't long before the men in uniform dragged her from the shed, toward Trenton Road where red and blue lights bounced off neighboring houses and bushes, filling the night with kaleidoscopic visuals she'd never forget.

EPILOGUE

(DREAMS MAY VARY)

10 months later...

From behind the doors of the capacious room where Angela Shepard sat at a long cafeteria-style table, staring at the wall and doing little else, Barry Harrison and a tall man with glasses, holding a clipboard, observed. Barry turned to the studious man, a doctor at the facility Angela had called home for the last ten months, the place where she had prepared for her trial and talked about her feelings and attempted to make sense out of what exactly happened.

"Think she's ready?" Barry asked the tall man, whose clip-on name tag read Daniel Stevens M.D.

Stevens seemed to consider the point. "As ready as she'll ever be."

"I hope she talks to me." Barry studied the woman who sat as still as a plush doll on a rocking chair. "I hope she accepts my offer."

The doctor didn't seem too keen on any of this, and he rotated toward Barry as if he intended to tell him so. "For the record, Mr. Harrison, I believe this is counterproductive to Angela's recovery. But, in saying that, I understand Dr. Rondo and the rest of the state board's decision to sign off on your waiver. I just wanted to interject my opinion before you proceed."

Barry waved his hand limply in the air. "Save it, kid. Just get me up to speed. What's she like? Coherent? Hopped up on crazy pills?"

Stevens paused, seeming unsure if he should answer. "Yes. Very coherent. She likes to talk. Although… she doesn't make much sense sometimes. She believes… well, very strange things."

"I bet." Barry checked his folder, making sure the proper paperwork and waivers were in order. "All right, let me in."

Stevens opened the door and gestured the television producer inside. Angela's head barely moved at the sound of the opening door. Stevens led Barry across the room, which was naked except for the long tables positioned throughout and a small tree staged in each corner, something Barry thought was used to calm the facility's patients and guests.

As he wandered across the meeting room, he studied Angela's face. She looked unwell and twenty years older than she had appeared on *Let's Switch Houses!* He could only imagine the volume of drugs they were pumping her with, and then wondered if that would somehow impact the signing of the legal documents he'd brought. *Is she even legally allowed to sign this under the influence?* He shook the thought away, claiming that was what the studio paid their lawyers for.

Barry took the seat across from her.

Stevens cleared his throat. "Angela," he said gruffly. "Miss Shepard?"

She perked up on the second request. "Yes?"

"You have a visitor."

"Oh?" She looked across from her. Seconds passed before a smile broke across her face. "Oh, Barry…"

"Hi, Angela. Long time."

"Barry…" she said thoughtfully.

He looked up at Stevens who towered over them. "Is she okay?"

Stevens shrugged. "Define 'okay.'"

"Is she…" He twirled his finger in the air next to his temple, and then pointed to the ceiling.

"High?"

"Yes."

"She's been given a light sedative to prevent one of her infamous episodes."

"Damn." He squinted. "Violent?"

"Extremely."

"Should her lawyer be present?"

"Probably."

Barry sighed. He felt his forehead grow hot. "Do me a favor. Please call him and tell him to get his ass down here. I don't feel like doing this twice."

"I'll see what can be arranged." He turned to Angela. "You and Mr. Harrison catch up, okay? I'll be right back. There are two guards just outside the room if either of you... need assistance. They're watching. Listening."

Barry didn't like the doctor implying anyone other than he could be in some danger, but he decided to let the comment slip. As soon as Stevens left the room, Barry rotated back to Angela and began sorting through the paperwork in his folder.

"How have you been, hon?" he asked.

She tilted her head and raised her hands above the table, showing off her collection of chains. "How the fuck do you think?"

"Yeah." He glanced around the room. "Not too cozy, I must say."

"I'm not crazy, you know?" She bit her lip. "They would have never made the switch, Barry. They would have never made it. Terry was wrong. They lied to him. Ester Moore lied to him." She leaned over the table. "You told me about Ester Moore. Who was she, Barry? What did she look like?"

He sat there, frozen. Ice water filled his veins, and a creeping chill cascaded down his spine. "I don't know, Angela. I just read about it online."

"Don't fucking lie to me, Barry."

He leaned back in his seat and looked back at the door. Shadows belonging to the guards moved behind the door's frosted window.

"Listen," he said, folding his hands on the table. "I hate to rush things along, but I really don't have much time. Your lawyer will be here soon and I doubt he'll let me have a word once he's here. So we have to be quick."

She nodded. "What is it you want with me, Barry? Haven't you ruined my life enough?"

Barry jerked his head as if she'd slapped him. "Ruined your life?"

"You set us up, didn't you? You made us swap houses with that woman."

Barry shook his head. "No, no. I didn't *make* you switch houses with *anyone*. That was *your* choice. I just presented you with an offer, just like I'm doing today."

She eyed the paperwork on the stretch of table between them.

Contracts. Lots of them.

"What is this?"

"I want to produce a new show. Starring you."

Her face remained unchanged. "What do you mean?"

"Well," he said, shifting in his seat, nervous energy pulsing through him. "I know you missed most of the entire season of *Let's Switch Houses!*, you know, being in here and such. But let me tell you—it was a huge hit, Angela. Big time. Ratings were through the roof, one of the best seasons we ever had."

She stared at him blankly.

"Anyway, I think a large part of the success was because of... well, you. And what happened. Current events. What you did—"

"Because I killed my husband and Rosalyn Jeffries?" Her eyebrows flared.

"Yes, partly because of that."

Her eyes slimmed so he could see nothing of her pupils. "Because of what I did with my son?"

Barry nodded slowly. "Yes. The public was very interested in your confession. *Obsessed* is probably a better word. It's the question that calls to them, you know."

Puzzled, her mouth fell to one side of her face. "What question?"

"Well... the why. *Why did she do it?*"

"I told them why."

"Yes, but that's not really the truth. The whole truth anyway. I think there's another reason why you gave away your son to a couple of complete strangers."

Tears populated in the corners of her eyes. She brushed her nose with the back of her hand. "Because... I... I couldn't deal anymore."

"That answer doesn't satisfy the public." He shuffled around the papers before him, and then dug through his breast pocket for a pen. "Plus, there was the search for William. The one your parents headed."

"The search?"

"Oh yes. They reopened the investigation and everything. For a while, it seemed like everyone in America was looking for your son. It was quite the hunt. I'm surprised your lawyer didn't fill you in. The doctors?"

"They don't talk about anything but my feelings and the case," she replied listlessly, tears streaming down her face. "Doesn't matter what they do. They'll never find him."

He glanced up from the papers. "No, they never did. In fact, they gave up after a few months. Trail went cold. Actually, the trail was never really warm to begin with. There are a few groups out there, real fans of the show, who still search."

"How is he?"

The question took him by surprise. "How is who?" he asked cautiously.

"My other William."

Barry's eyes slid back and forth. "What other William?"

She eyed him closely. "The one I gave birth to six weeks ago."

His eyes shot open. "Ohhhh. Yes. That. I almost forgot. The doctors did mention that to me."

"How is he? Where is he? Is he with family? No one will talk to me about it."

Barry folded his hands again, set them back down on the table. He sighed deeply, like a parent ready to dole out a severe punishment. "I know this is hard to hear, though, I suspect it's not the first time you've been told, buuuuuut… there was no other William."

Scoffing, she shook her head. "No, that's not possible."

"I'm afraid it is," Barry said. "I hate to say this, but you were never pregnant."

"No, I was. I was pregnant. I gave birth to another William. I remember it very clearly. The delivery went very well. No problems. Unlike the first time."

"It's all part of your psychosis, I'm afraid. You never had a second child. That day when you killed your husband and Rosalyn Jeffries, the authorities found pregnancy tests all over the bathroom. Thirty-seven I think the number was. All of them used. All of them showing negative results."

"Terry saw it. He made me take it. He showed me the results. They were positive."

"You're wrong, Angela."

"No, we were supposed to switch. The old William for the new. That was what Terry said; it was his idea. Ester Moore got to him. He killed Rosalyn Jeffries, Barry. Terry killed her because she was trying to help me—"

"Angela, your husband wasn't at Rosalyn's house that day. Only you were. He was at work. There were witnesses. Your DNA was all over the house. The mug of tea she gave you was all the evidence they needed."

"No, he admitted it, Barry. He told me he did it."

"You made it up, Angie. You made it all up in your head. You snapped after you saw the first episode of *Switch!* The guilt of what you did with your son was too much. You snapped, killed Rosalyn Jeffries, killed your husband, and here we are. I suspect if you weren't chained to the floor, you'd probably kill me too."

"No…"

"I'm sorry. It's true. Every word of it."

Catatonically, she stared at the man across from her. Her lips wriggled, unable to help produce any sounds.

"I know this is tough. I know your mental state of mind is fragile. So, let's get to it. I want you to tell your story. To America. I've gotten permission from both state and federal officials to let us film portions of the trial. We also secured permission from the board of doctors at this facility, and they are giving us full access to you. Twenty-four-seven surveillance. All we need, Angie, is you. You can set the truth straight. I know you have a story to tell. About why you did what you did. To William. To your husband. About what happened in your house after the show. I know you have a story burning you up so badly you can't sleep, can't think, can't eat. I know you need to purge. I know you need it, Angela, so…" He extends the pen in her direction. "…sign this. Please. We can help you with your trial, help you plead insanity. The studio has the best lawyers on the planet. Sign with us. We can help you get through this nightmare."

She accepted the pen. "They'll really listen to what I have to say?"

Dollar signs flashing before his eyes, he nodded. "Every word, sweetheart."

"Even if it sounds crazy?"

"Especially if it sounds crazy."

As she put the ink to paper, her face developed a spreading smile.

———○———○———○———

After she signed her life away, she glanced up at the ceiling. There was a small hole cut in the plasterboard, no bigger than a golf ball. She swore she saw an eyeball there, human flesh around the blinking orb.

She closed her own eyes, counted to ten, and opened them again, just like her team of doctors instructed.

The hole remained, but the eye was gone.

EPILOGUE II

(FAMILY MATTERS)

2 months later...

M a-me," the boy said, removing his eye from the hole in the bathroom wall.

"Honey?" a voice called from somewhere close. "Honey, where are you?"

"Ma-me." The boy looked at the hole with little emotion. There was a moment of hesitation where he thought he might return his eye to the hole to see what it would show this time around. "Ma-me."

"Honey?" The voice was behind him now. Footsteps knocked on the wooden floor of the hallway.

The boy turned.

A figure stood in the doorway, shoulder resting against the door jamb. "There you are, mister."

The boy looked back at the hole.

"What is that?" his mother asked. "Looks like this house needs a few repairs, huh?"

Mother had a peek inside the wall. She smiled. "Well, this house is just full of surprises. Isn't it?" She winked.

"Ma-me."

"Yes, mommy will have this patched up in no time."

More footsteps, the trampling kind, sounded up the stairs and down the hall. An out-of-breath woman appeared in the doorway, holding her chest and swallowing air. "Sweet Lord!" she said. "I'm so glad you found him."

Mommy patted her son on the head, kissed his cheek. "Yes. He's quite the wanderer. You never know where he'll end up next."

The woman in the doorway smiled. As she regulated her breathing, she rifled through her purse, removing a whole stack of stapled paperwork.

"Well, we must hurry. We have three more houses to hit before noon. I think the next—"

"That won't be necessary."

"Ma'am?"

"We're going to put in an offer on this one."

The real estate woman shot her an odd glance, and then surveyed the walls, their filthy condition. "Are you sure?" she asked, with a forced, fading smile.

"I've never been more certain about anything in my life."

With her smile completely gone, the woman set her house-hunting itinerary down on the sink. "Mrs. Wilson," she said, averting her eyes and pulling at her lower lip with her teeth.

"Please," Mommy said, grinning, "call me, Abbie."

"Abbie," the woman said, manufacturing a smirk. "This house… it has a little bit of a history, as I'm sure you know."

Grinning, Abbie nodded. "I know it well."

"Then, I must insist—why are you so keen on purchasing this home?" She winced as if the answer might inflict pain. "I can't even get people to drop by during an open house. I've tried everything. Cupcakes. Gift card giveaways. I even offered coupons for free massages. Nothing works. And then here you come, calling me out of nowhere, asking to see 44 Trenton Road in Red River, and—I'm just a little baffled, that's all, Miss Wilson—I mean, Abbie."

Abbie's grin widened. "I understand." She patted her son's head. "I guess this place just feels like home to us."

The woman glanced over at her son's expressionless face, then back to Abbie. "Okay," she said, finding a smile that passed as genuine. "Okay then, let's do this!"

Abbie smiled, laughed a little.

The real estate woman smiled, laughed a lot.

Abbie looked down at her son. "We finally found our home, William. We're finally here."

William looked up at his mother, Abbie Wilson, who went by many names, the woman who once called herself Ester Moore. Then, he returned his lazy gaze to the hole in the wall. "Ma-me," he said. "Ma-me."

"That's right," Abbie said, hugging the child. "You and Ma-me are finally home." She whispered into his ear, *The perfect place for all your brothers and sisters.*

The real estate woman didn't seem to hear this last part and waved them out of the bathroom, starting to ramble on about paperwork and how they should head back to the office and get started on their offer right away.

Abbie grabbed William's hand and led him out. Before they crossed the threshold and entered the hallway, William looked back over his shoulder, his eyes locking onto the hole on the far wall.

"Ma-me," he whispered.

That was all he'd ever whisper.

THE END

AFTERWORD

Every so often, my wife will pitch me ideas. Most of them are terrible (don't tell her I said that!). Sometimes—*rarely*—I actually like one. *The Switch House* started out like that. Late one night, she woke me up to tell me this "amazing" idea. It went something like this:

"A husband and wife go on one of those house-swap reality shows and when they come back, their house is haunted."

She told me all about the woman with whom they switched houses with, how she should be responsible for hexing their old home. I kicked the idea around for a couple of hours and put my own spin on it. I introduced the strained relationship between the husband and wife, the loss their family had endured and continue to deal with, and, of course, *the dream goblins*. She wasn't too keen on the latter. *No* supernatural elements was something she was very keen on. But, I didn't listen. I had already made up my mind—the dream goblins stay.

And so they did.

And I'm really happy with how it turned out. Her? Well, as of this writing, she hasn't read it yet. I suspect she will enjoy it, though it's not something I'd wager on.

I guess I'm writing this afterword to give my wife the credit she deserves. I mean, she deserves way more credit than just coming up with the plot for this story—after all, I constantly refer to her as the "glue" that holds our family together; without her, we'd all undoubtedly fall apart. So anyway, she came up with the framework and I fleshed out the characters, their motives, and I wrote the thing, and here we are. Even though my name is on the cover, she's definitely left her fingerprints on this one.

I had a lot of fun writing *The Switch House*. It was both familiar and unfamiliar territory for me. I feel the nature of Angela's "decision" was one of the darkest things I've written, and there wasn't a drop of blood spilled in that flashback scene. I enjoy a good kill scene as much as any horror fan, but sometimes the most terrifying stuff comes from the horrible decisions people make—especially involving the well-being of their children. Sadly, if you turn on the news, these stories will appear right in front of you. I can't think of anything more heinous, and I won't lie to you—writing *that* scene made me feel icky inside.

And that feeling is where the unfamiliar territory comes into play. Maybe I would have felt differently five years ago, before I was the parent of an autistic child. But now—no way. Icky all over. I shivered every second while writing it.

But I think that makes for the best kind of horror.

At least, I hope.

I'd also like to thank the following people who've helped in some way or another during the making of this book: Tim Feely, Matt Hayward, Chad Lutzke, Todd Keisling, Glenn Rolfe, Chuck Buda, and Curtis over at Cedar Hollow Reviews.

Also, a *special* thanks goes out to my wife for all she's done. I'll throw a big ol' THANK YOU to you, dear reader, for entering *The Switch House* with me. I hope you're not too changed by what you found here. However, if you do dream of alternate worlds between your walls, endless blue rooms occupied by the dead, and dilapidated houses that sit on the edge of nowhere and everywhere all at once—please don't blame me.

Blame my wife.

Cheers,

Tim Meyer
May 2018

BONUS:

SHORT STORIES

HOW TO KILL A BEAR WITH A BOW AND ARROW

Milo Medlock sat in a tree, the tallest oak in Red River, and waited for the bear.

He'd seen the report on TV last night; a black bear had been spotted sometime between six and nine, going through garbage cans on Southland Drive, near the bay. Three people reported the bear's presence, and one of them had stood on their porch and shouted at the beast, hoping the loud noises would spook off the bear. But it hadn't. According to the report, the bear had ignored all human requests and continued sifting through the garbage for edibles. Once it had finished, it hustled into the nearby woods, and no one had ever seen or heard from the beast since, though, the newscasters hadn't been shy about pointing out that the bear could reemerge any time it pleased.

Milo aimed his bow and arrow down at the ground. It'd been years since he'd shot the thing, and only dug it out for occasions like this. He wasn't ordinarily a hunter—he'd never killed an animal in his entire life, unless you counted flies and the occasional hornet. Never killed anything bigger than his thumb. But, when times called for it, when the neighborhood was under attack by bears or by criminals posing as post office workers, Milo Medlock grabbed his bow and arrow.

True story: About two years ago, Milo and his wife, Tilda, were watching the news one afternoon when a report came across the screen, informing the good people of Red River to be on the lookout for a dangerous criminal posing as a mailman. Apparently the scumbag was knocking on doors, pretending to deliver the mail, and then breaking into houses. Milo, not having a gun in the house to protect his family from the outside threat, had gone straight for the bow and arrow, the one his father had made him when he was just a small boy, almost forty years ago. Tilda thought the idea was ridiculous—she thought most of his ideas were—but she couldn't convince him to keep the doors locked and the windows shut instead of sitting on the roof and scoping out potential burglars dressed like mailmen.

"Just let the authorities handle it, you schmuck," she had told him. "Who do you think you are? Robin Hood?"

He'd told her that he obviously wasn't Robin Hood, but he was a pretty good shot. He'd practiced regularly in the garage with targets, beer cans and such. He'd never entered any archery competitions, but Roman—a friend from the office—always encouraged him to do so. But Milo wasn't the confident type and he never could bring himself to complete the online form for Red River's annual archery contest. He'd known how well he could shoot, but what if there was someone better? Someone more accurate? Someone who could split his own bullseye right down the center of his arrow, just like in the movies. He didn't think he could handle that kind of defeat. Even though he'd hit that mailman when he'd come strolling up the driveway with no car behind him, no sack of mail on his back, hit him right where he'd intended. Luckily, it *had* been the burglar, otherwise there might have been legal repercussions of his sure shot. He'd hit the thug right in the leg, through the calf, and made sure not to inflict a mortal wound. He could have if he'd wanted to.

If he'd wanted to.

If I'd wanted to, he thought, as he shifted in his makeshift tree stand. He was by no means a hunter, had never even given the sport any thought; something about killing innocent animals made him uneasy.

But what about the bear? Wasn't he innocent? After all, the bear hadn't done anything. Not really. It had invaded a suburban street and raided some garbage cans for food. It'd probably been hungry. It'd just needed some snacks. Something to get by on until something better came along. No harm in that. It wasn't a man-eater for Christ's sakes. It hadn't left the street a bloody mess of haphazardly strewn people parts. It had done nothing except to attempt to satisfy its most basic need—to eat. And it hadn't shed a drop of human blood to do so.

Not yet.

And that was where Milo Medlock drew the line. He wanted to remain proactive. Like the situation with the mailman imposter, he wanted to down the beast before it could inflict damage on the community. Sure, it'd started with a few overturned trash cans, but what came next? A few butchered people? Kids shredded like rag dolls on their way home from school? What if the animal wandered into that sixty-five and older community down the block? Granny might be watering her front lawn one minute, getting her fucking arm ripped off the next. Milo didn't need that. Not in his neighborhood. Not when he had the means to do *something* about it.

"You'll never kill that bear," Tilda had told him. "You don't have the sack." She'd continued to smoke her Marlboro Reds and watch Drew Carey on the television. She was only forty but she acted almost twice her age. Constantly nagging and crotchety. She'd been the reason Milo collected so much overtime, why he'd spent so much time in the garage with his bow and arrow and his almost-endless supply of Miller High Life.

"You said the same thing about the mailman who wasn't a mailman," Milo had told her. "Said I wouldn't get him."

"Not what I said, numb nuts." She'd scoffed then, between drags of her smoke. "Said you'd get yourself killed and unfortunately I was goddamn wrong about that."

"You know, you're a miserable wench, you know that?"

She'd ignored his comment, acted as if he hadn't said anything at all.

He'd leaned his head against the wall, and breathed in a cloud of second-hand smoke. He'd coughed something fierce and his asthma instantly flared. "Would it kill you *not* to smoke in the house? You know I have trouble breathing."

She'd flipped him the bird.

Sitting in the tree was peaceful. Milo breathed in the fresh atmosphere, his lungs full of healthy, clean air. It made him happy being alone. Happy to breathe. Happy to be amongst the silence of nature, those intermittent sounds of birds twittering and branches swaying, the swoosh of the wind passing through the trees. He closed his eyes and thought he was in heaven. He had no desire to head back, back home where hell waited.

⊸————◇————⊸

Milo hadn't any idea where to start. He'd watched a few Youtube videos on bear hunting but it hadn't seemed like a big enough sport. All the hunting videos featured deer or duck, and even less of them featured the bow and arrow. Everything was shotguns or rifles *(mostly rifles)* and those videos bored him. How hard was it to put down an animal using a gun? Seriously. At close enough range, a kill was almost automatic with a gun. Pull the trigger and the gun delivers instant death. No skill there. Now, to kill with a bow and arrow, one needed to be close. Real close. But not too close. Especially to a bear. Too close meant your head was coming off. Too close meant instant death, *for you.*

Milo had found one bear hunting video he liked and had watched it several times. One of the things the video preached was making sure to procure the proper license. Bear licenses were issued at certain times of the year depending on your State, and the instructor of the video told him not all states allowed bear hunting and to check the local gun shops for more details. Milo had done his research; New Jersey allowed black bear hunting and, sure enough, black bears were in season. He'd gone down to the local Waldo-Mart and gotten himself good and registered.

He was now licensed to kill... *bears.*

"Bet you're after that black bear everyone keeps talking about," the guy behind the gun counter had said to him.

Milo had nodded.

"Well, good luck, partner. Got any bait?"

"Bait?" The question had caught Milo by surprise. "What do you mean?"

"Need bait to catch a bear." The gun salesman had shrugged. "How else you gonna get that close?"

Milo hadn't thought about bait. He'd thought he'd peruse the forest that bordered Red River and hopefully pick up the garbage-sniffer's trail. That was what the Youtube video had taught him to do. Bait hadn't crossed his mind.

Now, in the tree, he looked down at his bait. It was a good choice, he thought, and he wondered if anyone else would agree. *Probably not,* he thought, smiling.

"Don't worry," he called down. "That bear'll be along soon and this will all be behind us."

His bait stifled a cry and called something back, words which were ignored. He'd heard something rustle amongst the leaves, and when he looked down in the direction of the sounds, he spotted a cluster of green foliage bouncing back and forth. Something had disturbed the shrubbery, something big.

Sure enough, a second later, a snout emerged from the forest. A massive, fur-covered cranium followed. Behind that, the bulk of the black bear came into view. It was bigger than Milo had expected, and, even from his vantage point, he could tell the beast was above average. In fact, he didn't think black bears grew to be that big. Its girth surprised him. No wonder the neighborhood had been shaken; if he'd seen that thing digging through his trash, he might have given this bear hunt idea a second thought. Suddenly the bow and arrow felt weightless in his hands.

The black bear moved out from the brush and into the clearing slowly, waddling back and forth, reminding Milo of the Youtube video. The bear in that video had been equally sluggish and in no rush to go anywhere. Milo thought that might change when the arrows began to fly, but he wasn't so sure. He didn't know how many it'd take to down the beast, but he'd brought two full quivers, twelve in each. He was hoping to only waste one arrow—hit the monster right between the eyes.

The monster.

The bear.

Were they the same thing?

Then the screaming started.

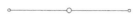

"OH MY GOD!"

Milo wished he'd put duct tape over her mouth. It would've been better that way, but he had needed something to grab the bear's attention. He couldn't risk it passing by without noticing the bait. He needed it close. He needed it practically on her so all he had to do was look down and fire. Shoot. Release the arrow, and watch it penetrate the skull right between its eyes.

The bear spotted Tilda and Tilda started screaming, really letting him have it.

"GET ME OUT OF HERE, MILO! GODDAMMIT! YOU SON OF A BITCH! I KNEW I SHOULD HAVE LEFT YOU! YOU WORTHLESS, LIMP-DICK FUC—"

The bear jumped back on its hind legs and roared. The bestial vocalization moved birds from their positions in the trees. It silenced Tilda at once. It gave Milo a rush of adrenaline and coated his skin in gooseflesh.

All of a sudden, things felt real.

There was no going back now. He aimed with his bow and arrow. He held his concentration on the bear's massive target of a head. The beast lowered itself down on all fours. It jogged toward the potential meal tied to the tallest oak tree in all of Red River.

Milo waited.

"HELP ME!" Tilda cried.

The bear approached, closing the distance with more speed than Milo had anticipated. The gap between his wife and the black bear slimmed. He looked down the arrow, picturing what it'd look like buried in the beast's skull.

The beast.

The monster.

Which one?

When the bear was about five feet away from Tilda—Tilda who now screamed and cried and begged to continue on with her lethargic lifestyle—the bear roared again, pushing the hair back off the face of its next meal. The bear took the last five feet in a slow, calculated approach. It sniffed its food before attempting to eat it.

This is good, Milo thought. This hesitation on the bear's part would allow him to adjust slightly, allow him to ready his shot, steady his aim. He did so accordingly, making sure he wouldn't miss on the first attempt.

But when he was ready to release the arrow, let his fingers slip off the string, he found himself unable to do so.

The bear sniffed under Tilda's blouse. She whimpered and turned her head. Then she screamed when the bear opened its jaws and bit down on her thick thigh. It tore away a section of meat, a slab of raw muscle.

Tilda screamed until her vocal cords broke.

Milo continued to sit in the tree, keeping his aim on the bear, but as time slipped, so did his view on the current situation. He'd come here to kill a bear. A beast. A plight on society. Something that terrorized and killed; something that must not live for the safety and well-being of others.

But that wasn't the bear, was it?

The bear hadn't hurt a soul, not until it had met Tilda Medlock, the real beast, the real monster in Milo's life.

The bear ate a piece of the woman's thigh and decided it deserved seconds. It lunged forward, snout first, and tore away another piece of Tilda's leg, from her calf this time. She thrashed around and cried out, but she was no match for the all-powerful jaws of the woodland critter. It feasted on her muscle, wrestling with the blood and skin, digging its nose deeper into her, pulling away with more gore and muscle, more pieces of Tilda.

Milo thought he should look away. He thought he should do something, other than sit in the tree stand he'd made for himself, his front-row seat to his wife's evisceration.

He decided he should end the beast's life.

He readjusted his aim and let the arrow fly. It connected true with a wonderful *THWACK!*

He wouldn't need another arrow.

The beast was dead.

And the bear continued to eat.

SIREN'S END

Clenching fistfuls of wet sand, the man climbed his way up the beach. Behind him, the waves clapped against the shore, sounding like the duel of distant pistols. Rallying against the pain, he forced his head around and glared at the ocean, the rocky sheet of endless gray. In that moment, somewhere beyond his vision, he heard his men scream, deck boards crack, and disturbed waters growl.

Was it the waters that growled? he thought, looking up, spotting the sky and noticing it held the same colorless hue as the ocean—here, the world looked dead. *Was it really the waters?*

Or something else?

When he couldn't take any more of the dismal scenery, he returned to his long crawl. Up the beach, a stretch of dunes blocked his vision of the deserted coastal town, a place he'd been before, a place that ended up not being deserted at all. There was one place that had kept its lanterns lit—a small pub about two streets in from the dunes.

If I can make it, the proprietor will help me. He had to. It was the least he could do. *He'll nurse me back to health and then...*

And then what? The survivor had no ship; that had gone down in a glorious battle with the sea and...

Those things.

Whatever they were.

He had no outs. He was trapped here. On this godforsaken edge of the world. This little island off the coast of the mainland.

The survivor managed his way up the beach, writhing like a worm through the sand, kicking his legs in rhythm with his upper torso. Surprisingly, the dunes weren't hard to summit. He'd reached the top and scouted the first avenue he'd set his eyes on, located his bearings, and then decided which course to take.

He slid down the dunes on his bottom. When he reached the stony, uneven road below, he tested his feet. His knees wobbled with the slightest bit of pressure. He sat back down. Five minutes later he tried again. Better this time. Easier. Less wobble in his knees, less ache in his bones. Not perfect. He spent another quarter hour standing, allowing his muscles to acclimate. It felt like he hadn't stood in years.

How long had it been?

He didn't know how long he'd been drifting in the Atlantic, floating among the flotsam of his ruined ship. Days? Weeks? None of it mattered now. His life—the only precious thing he had left to worry about. What little of it remained.

He hobbled down the street, toward the small inn/pub combo. He took the cobblestone walkway two steps at a time, paused, and then took two more. This approach ensured his body would not become overtaxed. His muscles protested movement of any kind, and hot flares of pain streaked up and down his body. He longed for the comfort of a mattress and pillow, the warmth of a hot compress and kindling in a fireplace. Tea. Yes, lots of tea. The phantom aroma of a hot cup filled his nostrils and that alone was enough to keep him warm for the time being.

A half hour later, the survivor found himself before Siren's End, the last pub on the edge of the world. He glanced around the dead street, remembering the days when this seaside town hadn't been so derelict, when townsfolk of all kinds populated these streets, bustling about their day. Those days were long gone, and it had been years since the shops around Siren's End had seen business, save for the pub and their occasional visits from passing fishermen and semi-lost seafarers. The occasional crew of adventurous pirates.

Now, everything here was closed.

Everything here was dead.

Except for Siren's End.

And Garrett Means, last captain of the King's Folly, aimed to find out why.

The buildings he passed were covered in soot, the fires that caused their condition long since smoldered. Debris littered the streets; old newspaper pages blew across his path, wooden slots from ruined crates and rum barrels lay across the cobblestone walkways, and spoiled food lined the gutters, too rotten even for the rats to claim.

A town in utter ruin.

When he arrived at Siren's End, he marveled over the impeccable condition of the inn's exterior. Fresh paint coated the brick facade. Black smoke unfurled from the chimney, suggesting the fireplace was in peak working condition. Gulls circled the sky above, hoping to secure fresh scraps from the kitchen.

Captain Means heard nothing from his position. The place seemed quiet on the inside, along with the apocalyptic town it resided in.

This dead city on a dead island off the coast of—if what Means had witnessed was any inclination—a future dead country.

Means headed for the door and was surprised to find the entrance unlocked. He shouldered his way inside, stood in the open doorway for a moment and took in the sights of the interior décor. It was as nice as any other pub along the coast. A place nice as this should have packed in quite a crowd, but today the joint was empty. Not a single patron was cozied up at the bar or occupying the nearby tables and Means suspected the inn's check-in log would prove every available room vacant.

Behind the bar stood a shadow.

"You've returned," the barkeep said, drying a drinking glass with a dirt-smudged towel. "With far less company than when last we met."

Tempted to rush the man, Means controlled himself, harnessing his raw emotions. He was in no condition to fight. No condition to take another step but he did so anyway, fending off the dizzying lightheadedness that crawled throughout his skull, erasing his worldly perception as it circumnavigated his dome.

"You..." Means managed to say, continuing his little two-step toward the closest stool. "You..."

"Yes, me. I know. A bastard, ain't I?"

"Did you know? Did you know she was among them? My Isabella? My sweet?"

The elderly man scratched his thick mutton chops with his free hand. "Isabella? Isabella?" He squinted. "Yes, I seem to remember an Isabella. Your sweet, you say?"

"You know damn well. I told you we were searching for her during our first arrival at this godforsaken place."

"I recall, yes, I recall."

"Where is she now?" Means put out his arms, resting his palms on the edge of the bar. He didn't know how long he could support his weight like this—maybe a few seconds—and then lifted his leg so he could plant his rear on the cushioned stool. His other leg couldn't handle the shift in weight and gave out, causing him to fall to the floor.

The barkeep heehawed. Another gut-shaking outburst followed. "Sure are a persistent bastard, aren't ya?"

Harnessing a few shreds of strength, Means rolled over. He faced the barkeep, the reason his brain would manufacture nightmares for every sleep to come. His lips parted, revealing teeth as yellow as a ripe banana. More laughter came from the insidious proprietor; it echoed in the empty chamber that was Siren's End.

"You fed us to those things," Means said, his lips stinging with a numb sensation. He sat up, his spine feeling like it had separated in several places. "You... sent us to that island."

"Aye, I did." The barkeep was pleasantly okay with this fact, causing Means cheeks to burn with indignation. "If it's any consolation, I take no pleasure in feeding them. They mean nothing to me."

A lie. A bold lie. His smiling face told Means that he enjoyed the arrangement very much. *Too much.*

"You're a liar. A traitor to the Royal Navy."

The barkeep shrugged. "Perhaps. Perhaps, my boy. Perhaps."

Means felt a surge of energy flow through him, and he launched himself to his feet. The sudden movement caught the barkeep by surprise. The man's eyes flared, his lips naturally forming a tight oval. He backed away, seemingly expecting Means to clamber over the bar and begin his assault, a barrage of blows that would leave him bloody or worse. *Dead,* dead like the islands his little monsters ruled.

"Do I scare you, old man?" Means asked.

The barkeep didn't respond. He stared at Means, holding the dirty glass out in front of him like a pointy knife.

Means bared his teeth. "I should kill you."

The barkeep's rigid expression broke, and his twisted smile returned. "You won't hurt me. You won't dare. You've seen what the women are capable of."

"You are a devil."

"Of sorts."

Means couldn't believe what he was about to ask. "What sort of devil are you?"

The barkeep brayed with more laughter, a deafening outburst that threatened Means's eardrums.

"Man," the barkeep said, his voice barely above a whisper. "The worst devil of them all."

---

40 Hours Ago

A pillar of fire in front of him and Means realizes the fore mast is burning. He turns and realizes the main mast has been set aflame, too. His men are scurrying across the deck, searching for either means of escape or recovery. Judging from the chaos, it seems the latter isn't likely. Men are abandoning ship, jumping overboard head first into the rough waters below. The entire stock of rowboats has been deployed, already gone amidst the fog, the all-encompassing white glow that surrounds them all.

He quickly wonders how he ended up here. He remembers Siren's End, the barkeeper drawing them a map to the island located a little less than fifty nautical miles from where they had sat and drank ale, and ate until they slipped into mini comas.

An Island of Women, he had said, which, to men who'd spent a great deal of time on the sea and limited hours amongst the company of women, sounded heavenly. They had set course at once and sailed west, toward the location of this great mystery.

An Island of Women, Means remembers thinking. If Isabella is anywhere, she is there.

Without much effort, they found the island. They discovered the women. But what happened after was very far from what the crew had envisioned upon hearing the barkeep's tale.

What they had found there was death.

Means shakes away the haunted memory of their visit. If he wants to survive, he needs to focus on just that, not past tribulations. He pushes himself to his feet and scrambles toward the edge of the ship. He looks down into the turbulent waters, eyeing the majority of his cowardly crew. They're swimming in the water. No, not swimming. Thrashing.

They're not alone.

The women are with them.

Feeding on them.

Their screams echo across the sea. The encroaching fog envelops them. All that's left of them are their final cries for mercy.

Means turns back to the deck. The fire is out of control now, spreading down the masts, conquering most of the boom and the roof of the captain's quarters. His materials, most importantly the portrait of his Isabella and the diamond intended for her finger only, are most likely on their way to becoming char and ash. A tower of fire stands tall over the bow. There are minutes left before the flames will travel to the deck and burn away the last remaining lumber of the sinking ship.

There's no rescuing King's Folly. They say a captain should always go down with his ship, but that's not for him. He has a reason to live—he has Isabella. She's out there somewhere. Among the women. Among the chaos.

Maybe if I can convince her, he thinks. Maybe if I can show her how much I love her?

He hasn't yet, which is why she left in the first place, why she joined this secretive commune.

He thinks about hurling himself over the edge when he hears a voice call his name. It's soft and familiar, somewhat comforting despite the anxiety lacing his nerves.

"Garrett?" she says, and Means turns to her.

"Isabella?"

She's standing in the center of the deck, Her Majesty's torn sails ablaze above her.

"Isabella," he confirms. She doesn't look the same as she had seven months ago, before her disappearance. She still has her slender appearance, her gaunt face, the features prevalent in the poor and homeless, but there is something different. Maybe it's her gown, the stark white garment that covers every inch of her flesh, making her look more angel than woman. Maybe it's the blotches of blood around her mouth, the remnants of her last meal. Maybe it's the teeth, those sharpened twigs of calcium, those tools of carnage. Maybe it's her nails, long and curled like hawk talons. It's the combination of these atrocities that contribute to her altered visage.

The woman he loves is no longer the woman he loves.

"What... what happened to you?"

She smiles, her bloody lips curling at the ends. "I've been reborn."

"You've become a devil."

"No, Garrett." Her face grows with concern as she steps toward him. "No, not at all. I've found a new way of life. That old life wasn't for me. You know that."

"We would have been happy together. You and I."

She shakes her head. "No, you would have been happy together." She nods her head to the side and bends her knee, a courteous gesture that comes off more like a warning. "I told you the married life wasn't meant for me."

"Your father... he promised you to me."

Her posture stiffens; her features constrict. "I am promised to nobody."

"We had an accord."

"I am not property!" she spits, flecks of blood sent airborne. "I am not his to pawn! Like some basic treasure!"

The venom in her voice nudges him backward. He feels the deck's rails against his back.

"Isabella, I'm sorry."

"You men," she continues, pointing at him as if he's every man that ever lived. "You men take and you take, and you don't consider us. Our feelings. Our wants and needs. You make us live like slaves."

"No, Isabella," he says. His mouth is dry and cottony, and the words almost don't come out correctly. "I love you. You know I do. You have to know that."

"You smother us with your love."

Three shapes form in his periphery. Three women, all of them clad in the same white material, all of their faces stained the same red.

"You smother us with your affection, your ideas of the perfect life." The closer she gets to him, the tighter his throat becomes. "But you don't know perfection like I know perfection. You've never tasted the flesh and blood of men, of God's so-called greatest creation."

"Now hold on just a minute," he says, barely. Feels like someone is squeezing his vocal cords. "You're sick. I can help you. I can nurse you back to—"

"I don't need your help," she says, lunging for him.

Before he can react, her mouth is on his throat. A wave crashes against the ship, and a salty spray dots the back of his neck. The next thing he feels is his blood leaving his body via the gaping hole Isabella has created near his jugular. Squirts of hot blood run down his neck, underneath his attire, coating his chest and stomach.

"Good-bye, my love," she says with such disdain.

His heart breaks in two as he's flung overboard, and into the stormy waters below.

Means clasped his hands around his throat, feeling his way around every inch of flesh. His heart sank when his fingers danced over the open area where flesh and muscle should have been. The cavity was dry and deep. The crusty nature of the wound suggested his body had recovered from Isabella's bite and was on the mend. But the depth and size of the cavity concerned him. It was deeper than an ordinary bite, at least by an inch or two, and about the size of a clenched fist. It wasn't exactly the kind of trauma one recovers from, even with proper medical attention.

"Mirror," Means demanded hoarsely.

The barkeep had one handy behind the bar and brought it to him promptly.

Means discovered his reflection. His vision was immediately drawn to the missing flesh on his neck. His breath caught in his throat upon witnessing his disfigurement. Bruised flesh surrounded the crater in his throat, the same purple-black marking that covered most of his arms and legs. He gently patted the wound and found it numb, probably why he hadn't noticed it earlier.

The strength ran out of his fingers and he let the mirror fall on the bar top.

"Quite the wound, sailor," the barkeep said with certain admiration. "Injury like that could kill a man."

He'd thought about that. It was miraculous that he had survived.

"What were they?" Means asked, though he already knew the answer.

"They're sirens, sonny. 'Bout the meanest creatures on this side of the hemisphere."

"And you're their what?"

The barkeep squinted. "I'm their contact. I'm their caretaker of sorts."

The shadowy corners of Siren's End began to move.

The barkeep hung his head. "I'm their slave." He lifted his shirt to reveal a dozen of tiny bite marks, pockets of missing meat. "They're so damn hungry."

Means turned his attention to the moving parts of the room. Shadows closed in until the glow of the lantern reached their figures. They shrank back into the shadows.

"Light keeps them away most days," he said, covering his exposed belly fat with his shirt. "They won't kill me, though. Just feed off me when they want a little snack."

"Because you feed them much larger meals." Means gritted his teeth. "Men. Entire fleets of men."

"It keeps me alive." The barkeeper shook his finger at him. "You'd do the same in my position."

"This town? This island?"

"Ate their way through it in a few months." He sighed deeply. "Soon, there won't be any ships left in the Queen's Navy."

"What then?"

The barkeep shrugged. "The homeland. All of Europe."

"We have to stop them."

The shadows hissed.

The barkeep chuckled, an almost-silent vocalization. "There ain't no stopping them. They're determined." He continued to shake his finger at him like a parent dishing out a good scolding. "Men like you created things like that. Remember this. You fathered these beasts."

His memory recalled Isabella, not the beautiful creature she was but the wretched monster she'd become. "I couldn't have... I only wanted to love. *Her* love."

The barkeep scoffed. "Love... is a two-sided coin, my pathetic friend. Can't have unity without the other half present."

"You don't know me," Means told him, as it became increasingly difficult to breathe. Spotting the creatures in the darkened corners, his heart raced. They were waiting, biding their time.

"Enough of this meandering. You've made your choice, *captain.* You've doomed your ship, your men, all in the name of *love,* or your misguided views on the subject."

"Who are you to judge me?"

Leaning closer to the lantern on the bar, he shrugged. "No one. Just a man. Remember? Most dangerous devil there is." He smiled and then blew out the small flame that had kept the entire establishment aglow.

In the darkness appeared several pairs of eyes, too many to count. They were a radiant turquoise, bright like the Caribbean seas he'd explored when he was younger. The ovals were drawn to him. They sped forth at once, and quick, and when they arrived there was pain.

Means screamed the only thing that mattered, his lost love's name—"Isabella!"—as the creatures dug into him, drank his sanguine nectar, and separated his muscle from the bone with their hungry mouths.

APERTURE

Placing the film against the aperture plate, the old projectionist grumbled, to himself, words of indignation. He snapped the gate over the film, adjusted the framing, and then turned to face the control station positioned directly beneath the porthole. Looking out across the theater, over the Friday night crowd and toward the screen, he pushed the glowing green button in the center of the panel. The motor kicked on, drowning out the distant noise of anxious moviegoers and the collective hum of the other nine projectors. The platter system spun with life, all three in sync with one another, feeding the rollers seven reels worth of footage. The projectionist stepped away from his work, folded his arms across his doughy chest, and looked to his company, his new apprentice, the preppy-looking youngster whose face had been taken over by utter confusion.

"Um," the kid said, his eyes darting back and forth. "That was great and all, but I have no idea what you just did."

"Weren't you paying attention, numb nuts?" the hermit asked, wiping his dirty, oily hands off on a shop towel. Once he deemed them clean enough, he stroked his gray-streaked beard, combing loose the speckles of leftover Doritos. Shooting the kid a steely gaze, the projectionist moved away from the machine, seemingly satisfied with the way the print was running. "I just threaded the fuckin' thing for ya. Pay attention next time."

Rob Garland wanted to take the timid approach. He thought about keeping hush, *really* thought about it, but he only had a week to learn everything the old hermit knew about being a projectionist. Instead of remaining quiet, he cleared his throat.

"I learn better when I *do.*" He kept still in fear that sudden movement would cause the hermit to start chucking empty reels at his head.

"You'll *do*. You'll *do* plenty. Patience is a virtue. Doesn't your generation know any-goddamn-thing?" He didn't allow a response, which was fine because Rob knew the question was rhetorical. "Goddamn millennials. We're talking about threading a projector here, not splitting atoms. Come here. I want to show you the building station."

Rob followed the man over to the secluded area of the booth that consisted of a work bench with two circular disks angled outward, jutting pegs in the center where the reels were commonly placed. Compiling five to six reels into one massive print looked complicated—Rob had seen it done before—and he wasn't sure if he'd "get it" in only five days. No, it wasn't splitting atoms, but it might as well have been.

The projectionist pointed to the splicer sitting on the bench. "See that? That's your best friend. That's what we use to splice the frames together. Get it?"

"Uhhhh... sure."

"Good. I'll show you how to build a print on Wednesday when the new movies come in. In the meantime, we can splice together some trailers for practice." He nodded in the direction of the cage on the far end of the booth. "Let me show you where we keep some supplies."

"Yes, sir."

Before he took his next step, the old man shifted his gaze back to Rob, his eyes barely visible between his lids. "You call me sir one more damn time and Imma splice your chode off, cock boy. Got it?"

Snickering, Rob nodded.

"Now call me Dan, my fuckin' name, or suffer the fuckin' consequences."

"Yes, Dan."

Rob followed Dan to the cage, a small corner of the booth sectioned off by raw wood framing and chicken wire. Dan popped open the gate and led Rob inside. The cage was trashed with what Rob considered junk. There were Christmas decorations and old projector parts, cardboard boxes filled with rolled-up movie posters dating back to the eighties and dozens of empty reels. Rob also noticed several unopened canisters tucked away in the corner. There was some crap, various marketing materials that never made their way downstairs, cardboard displays and paper handouts, covering the orange and silver canisters, but he spotted them anyway.

"Okay," Dan said, kicking a path to the far wall. "Here's where we keep the trailers. We got a ton of old ones we keep for training thumbsuckers such as yourself. Here's one for *Pulp Fiction.*" He snatched the small hockey puck-looking disc off the shelf and held it to the light as if he'd discovered a blood diamond beneath the African soil. "You like Tarantino, kid?"

"He's all right," Rob replied, his eyes drawn to the corner and the canisters. "I mean, I like everything he's done, even though *Jackie Brown* was kinda boring."

Dan blew an irked breath between his lips and said, "Well, you're fuckin' boring" quietly, so Rob couldn't hear. But Rob did hear and only laughed at the crusty old bastard. "Nonsense," he barked, and continued to grumble on about kids and respect, and did so in near silence. "Anyway, have your pick. There are all types of trailers up here. Knock yourself out. I might take *Pulp Fiction* with me. Consider it my retirement gift from this piece-of-shit, no-one-gives-a-fuck-about-you place they call The Orchid 10."

"What are those?" Rob asked, pointing to the partially-hidden canisters.

Dan arched his brow. "Those?" He waddled over to the old dented cans and bent down on one knee. "Well, one of them is *Austin Powers and the Spy Who Shagged Me,* and the other..." He knocked over the marketing materials like the trash they were. They spilled across the floor, mixing with other throwaway items of little to no importance. The first thing Rob wanted to do when he took over Dan's job was to clean out the cage, make it look somewhat presentable. "The other is a rare print from my own personal collection."

"You collect prints?"

Dan rotated his entire body toward the kid. His lips carved out an almost sinister smile. "Yes. Yes, I do." A faint laugh lived and died in his throat.

"Mostly foreign flicks. Rarities and B-sides. Stuff you've probably never heard of, stuff you might not even find on the Internet. Stuff that may or may not sell for a fortune if I live long enough."

"What kinds of movies?"

Dan's forehead bunched together, creating wrinkles and ripples across his pale stretch of skin. "Do you like horror movies, kid?"

Rob shrugged. "Sure. Rob Zombie's first couple were good. I'll see the new one."

The projectionist scoffed. "Rob Zombie? The man wishes he could make the types of films I'm talking about. The types of films I collect are true masterpieces. They're true art. They're... how shall I put this?" He pressed the tip of his forefinger against his chin. His eyes expanded as the words came to him. "They are morbid perfections."

Rob stared at him, unblinking. "Oh-kay, then."

"Take this one for example." He popped the latch on the orange canister and pulled back the lid. Inside sat three reels. "It's a short flick. Only about an hour. French title. *Ouverture.* English translation: *Aperture.*"

"Like an aperture plate?"

Dan winked at him the way one might near the end of a flirty date. "Exactly. Guess you were paying attention after all. An aperture is an opening. In our biz, it's the space that allows light to pass through the projector, allowing the image captured on film to project onto the screen. In this film's case..." He stroked the reels as if they were the spine of his favorite cat. "...it's... well." He laughed incredulously. "Never mind, kid. You wouldn't believe me. Not a thing like this."

Rob folded his arms across his chest. He'd just turned eighteen and had learned a long time ago the difference between when someone was sincere and when someone was putting him on. But in this moment, he couldn't decipher if Dan was serious or yanking his cord. At the very least, the old, nearly-retired projectionist *believed* in what he was talking about. He'd known Dan for about a year, since he'd started working at The Orchid 10 last summer. He'd only spoken to the man a handful of times since, and he hadn't seemed *too* loony. A man of few words, sure, but not the bat-shit bonkers turd everyone made him out to be. The man was a hermit, a real recluse, and Rob didn't know him any better than he knew the guy at Wawa who brewed his coffee every morning.

"Try me," Rob said, his curiosity piqued.

Dan flashed him an excited, grinning look. "You want to see it?"

"Sure." He didn't know if he did or not, but the answer came forth anyway, as if there were no possible way he could stop it. "What's it about, though?"

Dan rubbed his hands together in delight. "Oh boy. You're in for a real treat. A *reel* treat," he said, snatching a reel out of the canister and holding it up to illustrate his pun. "It's a story about love and death. Life and what lies on the other side of death's door. Some say," he said, that sick grin still pasted across his face, "that one viewing will open up a portal in your mind, allow you to see what's on the other side. A temporal gateway of sorts."

"An aperture," Rob mumbled.

"Yes, kid." Grinning still, the hermit revealed gums that had blackened over the last sixty years. Teeth that were long overdue for repair, maybe past the point of restoration. "An aperture into another world."

"So you've watched it?"

He looked down at the reel in his hand. "Well... no."

"No?"

"No," he said confidently. "Why would I? That sounds scary as shit."

"You've never watched it?" Rob asked, almost angrily.

"No. Nope. Started to once. Got about five minutes in and had to shut it down. Gave me a headache something fierce."

"What happened? What was on it?" Rob felt his obsession with Dan's story grow, as if it were some living, palpable thing inside him. Feeding on him. Gnawing from within.

A crown of sweat dripped from Rob's forehead. He felt lightheaded.

"You okay?" Dan asked.

"Fine. Tell me about the print. What happened?"

Dan shrugged. "It was just too... bizarre."

"Isn't that *why* you'd watch it?"

"Listen, kid. When did this turn into an interrogation?" Dan put the reel back in the canister and shut the case. "I just collect the shit, hoping it sells when I retire. Which is next week, by the way. Which means you're going to be the new lead projectionist. Which means we need to learn your ass."

"We should watch it."

Dan's smile danced off his face. His color paled. "You... really... want to?"

"Yes." He'd called the old hermit's bluff. "Yes, let's watch it."

"Oh... oh, okay. Tonight then. Midnight. I'll thread theater one."

"Perfect."

He didn't know why, but midnight couldn't come fast enough.

The lobby of Orchid 10 was unsurprisingly vacant for a Monday night after the last show had gone in. Rob drifted toward the popcorn stand where the cute new girl stood behind the counter, prepping the popcorn popper for closing. She had already emptied it and was beginning to wipe down the greasy interior.

"Jumping on that a little prematurely, huh, new girl?" Rob asked, leaning on the candy counter.

She twisted her neck, continuing to spray down the stainless steel kettle. Flashing him a superficial smile, she said, "Dude, no one else is coming in."

The second the words left her mouth, a couple stumbled through the front door, holding hands and giggling. They asked Rob if they were too late, if they had missed any part of the movie. While staring at the new girl, he simply said, "No," and then proceeded over to the ticket booth.

"And be sure to try our number one combo," he said loud enough so the new girl could hear, his lips pressed into a devious smile.

The new girl scowled, but when the couple came over to order a number one, she greeted them like the training videos instructed. "Anything else?" she bubbled and they shook their heads "no" and headed for the theater.

"There's always one," Rob said, winking at her.

She wriggled her lips and returned to her closing tasks, starting the process from the beginning.

Rob leaned on the counter again, the lower half of his face barely able to contain his grin. "Always one—"

"Cram it, Garland," she said sharply. She turned to him and pretended to squirt cleaner at him, mimicking the squishy sounds it made when it shot from the nozzle. (*pshoo-pshoo*). She returned his goofy grin.

The two of them had been playing this little flirty game over the last week, basically since Brianne Welker's orientation. On her first day, she had told Rob that she had broken it off with her boyfriend and was looking forward to spending the summer before senior year single. He thought that info was a little too much to reveal on her first day, but he didn't mind; they had shared a strong connection from the second he had laid eyes on her, the second he had opened his mouth. Their first conversation felt like it would never end, be consumed by awkward silences or grow dull. They shared likes and dislikes and discovered they loved the same movies. They spent the rest of the afternoon cleaning theaters, discussing their favorite films, albums they'd require if stranded on a desert island, and which books they'd read over and over again. She was a little too much of a Harry Potter nerd for his tastes, but that was okay; he liked the books too and told her Universal was supposedly opening up a Harry Potter theme park, which she already knew about and claimed she'd be first in line when it opened next fall.

They talked for hours even though their exchange only seemed like minutes. And when the day was over, they continued their conversation via text message.

They next day they were making out in the ice room. Rob had her back pressed against the ice machine. She jumped up on his hips and wrapped her legs around his waist. It was a scene out of every romantic comedy he'd ever seen. They'd spent the next ten minutes swapping saliva until one of the other ushers had barged in. The usher's face had twisted with alarm and embarrassment, and he'd immediately thrown his arm over his eyes and backed out of the room.

Since then, they had made sure to carve out at least ten minutes of every shift to make kissy-face in the maintenance closet.

"What are you thinking about?" Brianne asked him.

"Nothing?"

Her eyes slimmed. Cocking her head, she said, "You're thinking about the broom closet again, aren't you?"

"No..." Rob winked and held the pose. "Okay, I was. Sue me. Wanna go?"

"I have to finish cleaning the popper. Then sweep and mop the stand. You know the routine."

"Yeah, I sure do."

"Plus, I was thinking we could do something else. You know, *besides* making out."

"Oh?" Rob perked up. His pants suddenly felt a little tighter. Sweat crawled down his inner leg. "Like what, pray tell, did you have in mind?"

Buffing the counter with a clean rag, she shrugged. "I dunno. Dinner? The diner on 37? IHOP? I'll even let you pay the bill."

"How gracious of you." Rob folded his arms. "Got a better idea. Dan just invited me to a movie tonight. A sneak peek."

Brianne's brow spiked with interest. "Oh? The new Nolan?"

He shook his head. "No, something a little more obscure."

She seemed almost disappointed.

"Some foreign film," Rob said, filling up the napkin dispenser. "It's French. *Aperture*, or something. Says it's supposed to be scary as fuck."

"Really?"

"Really."

"I do like French films. Ever see *Chocolat?*"

"No. God, no. And I don't plan on it either."

"It's so good. Plus, you know—Johnny Depp and stuff."

"Terrible." He slammed the top down on the napkin dispenser and tugged the first one through. "So... you in?"

"I don't know. Sounds weird. And creepy. And that guy Dan gives me the willies. He should invest in some deodorant."

"Come on. He's not so bad."

"He never comes down from up there. I met him once, my first day. I said 'hello' and he grunted something back that wasn't even English."

Rob squeaked with laughter. "Yeah, that's Dan. Man's a bit of a recluse. He's harmless. And a good guy once you get to know him. This theater will suffer without him."

Brianne finished the counter, and then bent over to put the lid back on the candy case. "Fine. We'll watch your French flick. But can we get food? Fuck, I'm starving."

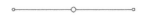

Two minutes to midnight and Dan Galloway had finished threading *Ouverture*. The sensation in his fingers while placing the film on the rollers had been too strong to ignore. They'd gone rigid a few times, especially while he'd fed the film through the brain, the piece stationed in the center of the print that controlled the speed of the platter. Numbness ruled his hands, down to the bone, every nerve shredded. When the tingling sensation abated, a shooting pain took its place and shot up his arm, needling his elbow. Nerves swam like a school of sharks in a feeding frenzy. His brain felt cloudy and empty, like a veil draped over his thoughts, preventing any original content from forming. He got the sense that, if he tried to speak, his words would come out as inarticulate syllables.

When finished, he took a seat next to the projector. He inhaled slowly, heard himself wheeze with each breath. A funny tingle fingered his heart, and he wondered if this was it, if this was the big heart attack that had ended many other Galloways before him.

He rested, but, as the seconds ticked on, he felt no better.

Eventually, he pulled himself up. Looking through the porthole, he spotted his protégé, the kid who'd replace him in a week's time, and the kid's new squeeze, the saucy new girl who served up one hell of a number two combo.

His lips spread into a smile, but the emotion behind the action quickly faltered. The realization of his successor's dim future hit him hard. His mood suddenly soured and he felt awful for Rob. In a few years, this job would be gone. What was once a pretty decent-paying job complete with benefits and union perks, would give way to part-time minimum wage work only. True projectionists were a dying breed and he was the last of his kind. Dan predicted digital hardware would replace film in two year's time, maybe less depending on the market. Soon, any two-bit numbskull with the brave ability to press a button could start a projector. Projectionists were trending toward obsolete, like the clockmakers and switchboard operators before them, and that bent Dan's smile, crushed his high spirits.

Dan pressed the green button. The motor buzzed to life. The rollers fed the film along. The lamphouse glowed bright, projecting images on the screen. Dan raised his vision and focused on the front of the theater. Some French words were written in white against a black background.

Dan felt a presence behind him. A figure. Standing tall in the booth, looming over him, stretching like some indefinable shape, free from the constraints of gravity and other earthly restrictions.

He turned and saw nothing. No floating shape. No dim, jellylike figure reaching for his neck. Nothing but shadows and the small cone of light looking down at his workstation.

Silly, he thought, *you're being silly.*

He returned to the film. The black and white images appeared before him, changing within a few seconds of showing themselves. They were of random things. Grotesque things. Things he'd seen before, once, when he first acquired the film from some junkie ex-actor who'd stolen it from some big-wig Hollywood executive twenty years prior. He'd made it about five minutes in before having to shut the damned thing off; he wondered how long he'd last the second time around.

The feeling returned. Something behind him. Some unspeakable horror, some gangrenous creature dripping with black, vile fluids, reeking of death and disease, a limitless mouth filled with tiny white shards of teeth, motivated to destroy and defile all that made the human world good and perfect, all that made it *human.*

Dan turned and expected to see nothing again, much of the same; the dim light and shifty shadows the projection booth usually harbored.

But what stood before him wasn't a trick the shadows provided. It actually resembled the horrors his brain conceived.

Only worse.

The thing was real.

After the first few minutes of random gross-out frames and still credits, the meat of the film began. Rob threw his arm around Brianne and pulled her close. The top of her head fit perfectly in the space between his cheek and shoulder, snugly, like there was no other head in the universe meant for that special place. They locked together and fixed their eyes on the screen, waiting for the story to unfold and sink its claws into them.

(The woman on screen was folding laundry. She sat on her bed, piling the squared articles on top of one another. She was crying but trying not to. Sniffling.)

The scene changed: a dead bird spattered against the dotted line on the asphalt surface, a feathery blob of bones and blood. A hammer coming down on a human hand, smashing the fingers into twisted extensions of flesh and exposed white. A woman hurling herself off the balcony of a sky-high tower and a few frames of the black, soupy puddle she'd become.

"What the hell are we watching?" Brianne whispered.

"I don't know," Rob said, feeling slightly disgusted, slightly amused. A cold wave crashed against his arms and legs, causing a layer of gooseflesh to sprawl over him. "Whatever it is, it's cool as fuck, though."

"Cool?" She pushed away from him, breaking contact. "This is sick."

Rob turned to her. "We can go if you want."

On screen, an army of spiders crawled over a woman's mostly-deteriorated corpse. There was no denying the corpse was real and not a prop. Rob felt its authenticity in his bones.

Brianne seemed to weigh her options in silence, as more unspeakable acts of violence were projected before her. Scenes depicting real-life mutilation flashed between brief moments of what might have been a cohesive, coherent story had the filmmakers stuck with it.

"No," she finally said. "But I need to pee."

"Okay." Rob looked around the empty theater. "If you see Dan, tell him to come join us."

She nodded, and then took off down the aisle.

He cupped his hands over his mouth. "And bring me snacks!"

She gave him two thumbs up.

Rob reclined in his seat and focused on the picture.

(The woman moved to the window, looking out across the street. Below, townspeople bustled. As she watched, the woman said something in French and there were no subtitles to accompany her voice.)

"What the hell are you making me watch, Dan?" Rob whispered to himself.

More quick scenes: a man getting hit by a car, a tire rolling over his head, flattening his cranium, coagulated lumps of brains and blood spurting through the cracked skull and split flesh. A pack of lions tearing into a zebra, ripping huge chunks of skin and muscle away, still alive as the predators quarter the defenseless, struggling animal. An entire hallway of flyblown bodies, the surrounding walls dripping with dark fluids. A homeless clown sitting on the street corner of some busy intersection, munching on a severed hand, while several pedestrians pass by seemingly unaware of the menace's existence.

(With her back to the camera, the woman faced the open window. The bustle of Paris faded into the background, reduced to faint white noise. She turned to the camera. The woman's face had changed, suddenly different. She had morphed into a different woman altogether. It was...)

"What the hell?" Rob asked the empty theater, pitching himself forward.

The woman on screen was no longer the Frenchwoman.

"Help me, Robbie," the woman said in a voice that no longer carried a French accent. It was American. It belonged to Brianne. "Help me, Robbie," the new girl repeated. "Help me." There were tears in her eyes, streaming down her face, running off her cheeks. But she didn't appear sad like he thought she ought to, rather, indifferent about the situation. Maybe not even that. Maybe... *happy?* He swore the ends of her mouth curled, traces of a smile beginning to take shape. "They're coming for you, Robbie. They're coming for all of us. They can't be stopped."

Rob launched himself out of his seat. He stood there, eyes glued to the black and white screen.

Brianne's body heaved as she began to sob. "They're coming." Her voice changed just then. Deeper. Several octaves lower. Eerily demonic. "They're coming. We let it out, Robbie. *We let it out."* The last sentence sounded like a record played backwards, low and warbled. *"We let it out! We let it out! We let it out!"* Her screams sounded like the howling gale of a bad storm. Her fists beat against the camera, shaking the frame. No, not the frame. *Him.* She was beating him. He felt the impact of her blows on his chest and shoulders.

Rob turned to run but there was only darkness behind him, an endless, lightless void. He thought about jumping into the inky lake before him, but there was a sense of threat there, a notion that this was darkness not to be trespassed, that there was no return from this place. This was a place that kept *things*, his intuition told him. There was no coming back.

No coming back.

No coming back!

He turned back to the screen and faced Brianne, who was now standing in the row before him dressed in the Frenchwoman's attire, that silky satin robe.

"NO COMING BACK!" Brianne shouted in a voice that wasn't her own, and possibly belonged to some foul soul residing in the deepest depths of Hell.

Rob backed away as Brianne's mouth remained open, displaying rotted teeth, a tongue comprised of writhing maggots, which spilled over her lower lip as she continued to shout. *"NO COMING BACK! NO COMING BACK!"*

Rob jumped backwards expecting to clear the seat, but there was nothing left of the theater behind him except the dark abyss. Icy hands grabbed him and pulled him under, taking him to—

Rob flailed and cried out. Gasping for fresh air, he lunged forward. Brianne screamed and jerked the wheel, causing the tires to wail beneath them.

"What the fuck, dude?" she asked, flipping off the horn-honking driver to her left.

"I'm sorry," Rob said instinctively. "What-where? Where am I?"

"Um, you're in my car. On the way to IHOP. Like we said. Like two minutes ago. Before you passed out and went all *Jacob's Ladder* on me."

Rob wiped a layer of cold sweat from his brow. "I thought... the movie."

"What movie? *Jacob's Ladder?*"

He shook his head and suffered a sudden wave of dizziness. He fought off the urge to puke all over the glove box. "The one we were watching." He swallowed and tasted acid, the bile in the back of his throat. "The French flick."

"What the hell are you talking about?" She took turns between eyeing him warily and concentrating on the road. "We left work and decided to go to IHOP. There was never any movie."

"No," he said, shivering. A fever worked over him, and he could feel a sickness crawling through his veins, infecting each organ as it traveled deeper and deeper into his body. The sudden notion to rip his hair out became strong, and he found himself fingering around his scalp. "No, we were watching..."

"Are you feeling all right?" She felt his forehead. "Jesus, you're burning up. Maybe I should just take you home."

"No. Home." The highway lights became a shifting kaleidoscope of bright colors. He took another spin on the fever carousel.

"Fuck that," she said.

"No." But he had no choice in the matter. She had already pulled off the main drag and was heading down Green Street, toward Rob's parent's house.

The next morning he felt much better, at least physically. He went to work with his head in a cloud, his brain polluted with weird thoughts, but his body felt all right. He wasn't hot or sweating pellets of ice; he was good. But his head, on the other hand, felt like someone had set off a fog machine in there, pumping ghostly images of things that should not exist directly into his mind's projector. He tried to remember the previous night in its entirety; the film, what happened during the viewing, the bizarre events that had followed. But he couldn't do it. It wasn't there, not all of it. There were fragments, just pieces. Broken images and shattered visions. Tidbits of a good bad dream, there somewhere beyond the veil of reality. Enough to verify what he'd seen was real, but enough to doubt its authenticity.

When he arrived at work, he decided what had happened last night was real. The film was real. The viewing was real. Everything that had happened was real right up until he'd awoken in Brianne's car, screaming like a newborn baby thirsting for the teat.

But what was real?

The movie he hardly remembered?

The reels in his mind began to spin, projecting the Frenchwoman while she pleaded for help. But it hadn't been her, right? No, it had been Brianne.

He remembered the sick, nasty scenes spliced between those involving the Frenchwoman. Yes, it was all coming back to him. Slowly. Fragments. Dirty, twisted concepts weaving together like fine threads until they had come together and become one complete garment. The closer he got to the projection booth, the more he remembered. By the time he passed theater six, he had recalled everything.

He found Dan sitting behind his desk, awkwardly slumped. He lifted his head from the blank wooden space before him, and smiled. His teeth had seemingly rotted completely black overnight. His eyes and the tone of his skin had yellowed with jaundice. Most of his hair had fallen out, leaving behind noticeable patches of scalp. A dozen or so clumps of silver strands remained.

Dan coughed. "You like the movie, kid?"

Rob had approached with no apprehension, but once he set eyes on the old projectionist, he found himself backing away. "What happened to you?"

"I watched it," he said with a bright smile. "I finally watched it."

"Jesus, your face."

"My face is beautiful." He touched a spot on his face where a boil had formed. The tumor-like growth had filled to the point where Rob thought it might break and discharge pink, toxic juices. "I'm transforming. Becoming one with the other side."

"What other side?" Rob trembled. "What are you talking about?"

Leaning forward, Dan squinted. "You didn't see it? You didn't stare into the abyss?"

"I saw..." What had he seen? He remembered gazing into the black and seeing nothing but the endless void. "I saw nothing."

Dan shook his head violently. "Oh no. You saw what I saw. You saw into the aperture. Into the dark world. And you know what?"

Rob was too terrified to respond.

"The dark world saw *you.*"

He wanted to turn and run, but fear rooted him to the floor.

"You can't run," Dan said as if he'd read the kid's mind. "You can't outrun what is everywhere. The dark world is everywhere now, hidden behind the veil of our own precious domain. There. Hidden. Waiting. Gaining traction. The film," he nodded to the three reels sitting on the desk, "will be shown to the masses."

Rob found enough courage to speak but he was still trembling. "N-no. It can't."

"Yes, it can. And it will."

"W-we can stop it."

"Too late. Darkness is like wildfire; it spreads quickly. And this film is pure darkness."

"P-please."

"Go now," Dan suggested, sweeping the three reels closer to him so he could rest his head on them. "Go and live your life. What's left of it. Live until the darkness catches up with you. It's not far behind. In the meantime, I will protect the film, as I always have." He perked up. "Funny, how I've never watched it before. After all the years I've had it in my possession, I picked now to view it. Curious."

Rob thought it was curious too, but kept quiet. Too many of his thoughts were bumping into each other, fumbling.

"I never watched it until I met you," he added, before putting his head back down, where it would remain for a good long while.

Rob went downstairs, handed in his immediate resignation, and walked out the doors of Orchid 10 for the last time.

He thought he felt a cold darkness saunter after him and follow him into the parking lot.

———◇———◇———◇———

Rob grabbed the door handle and pulled.

"Where do you think you're going, hot stuff?" Brianne asked from behind him.

Rob turned, and the sudden movement brought a sickly sensation to his stomach. Brianne strolled toward him casually, twisting her body with each step. Overhead, roiling gray clouds closed off the sky. The atmosphere reeked of damp air. Rain was on the way. Lots of it.

"Didn't think you could quit and not say goodbye to me," she said with a friendly, welcoming smile that almost erased his uneasiness. "Did you?"

"I was gonna text you."

"Sure you were." She stopped a few feet away from him. "You okay? You've been acting weird. First last night, now, you quit your job? It's not me, is it?"

"No, definitely not you."

"What then?"

Rob knew what it was—*that goddamn movie.* He couldn't bring himself to speak the words aloud. "Nothing. Just going through some stuff."

She clicked her tongue. "Got it. Say, wanna take a ride with me?"

He glanced around the half-vacant lot thinking he shouldn't, how he should go home instead and wait for Dan's darkness to slither over him like a bucket of poisonous snakes.

"Sure, why not."

"Follow me," she said, almost seductively.

He did.

When he plopped himself down on her front seat and shut the door, he felt better. Not perfect, but better than he had only minutes ago. Like he'd shut out Dan's darkness. Brianne's car acted as a safe place, a haven from the unnamable things released by the foreign film.

"Where are we going?" he asked.

She pulled out of the parking lot, onto the main drag. "I dunno. For a drive. We never got that IHOP dinner you promised me."

"I'm not hungry."

"No, I wouldn't imagine you would be." A horde of invisible spiders crawled down his arms. "With everything you've witnessed."

He snapped his head in her direction. "What?"

She smiled. Grinned. Much like Dan's jaundiced face had.

"Did you like my movie?" she asked. "I made it for you, you know."

"Wha-what?"

"Well, not *you* specifically. The children like you. My little puppets. There have been so many of you over the years." She giggled, a high-pitched noise that sliced open his nerves. "My little agents of darkness."

Rob went for the door handle but the child locks were already on. He tried to push the button, but it didn't move. He elbowed the window but the glass held, held through each violent effort.

"There's no escape, little one," she said, the lower half of her face complete with a crescent smile. "Did you know the Frenchwoman was my birth mother? Bet you didn't. That's a fun piece of trivia for you. One you won't find on IMDB. Though, you won't find *Ouverture* on there, either. Will you?"

No, he didn't think he would.

"What are you?" he asked, squeaking the words out.

"Oh, a little of this. A little of that." She let her head fall sideways and set her eyes on him. He stared back, looking into the shimmering black orbs that filled in her irises. "My kind are the creators of the void. And I'm its keeper. Its protector. Its mother. Like my mother before me and hers before her. And, like all good mothers, we need to feed our babies."

Her eyes were normal again, bright as two blueberries.

Rob could barely speak, his windpipe feeling about as wide as a drinking straw. He croaked. "W-what d-did you make us watch?"

"Just a film. One of my favorites."

"That wasn't *just a film.*" Rob felt weak, barely able to move. His thoughts began to bleed away. "What... was it?"

She shrugged. "The void needs to feed, and there is nothing more nutritious than the human noggin. Not the outside, of course. The shell is too bony and tasteless. But what's on the inside, what exists within the brain, where thoughts and imaginative cognitive skills are brewed—now that's the ticket. One human imagination can sustain the void for a thousand years, which is a long time for your kind, but, in the grand scheme of the megaverse, it only equates to about a day or two in Earth time."

"Why... me?" Rob felt all strength abandon his limbs. As he wasted away, he looked into the sideview mirror and saw his features had yellowed, grown overripe with jaundice. "Why..."

Brianne, or the thing she truly was, shrugged. "Because you were easy. And the film was here. Dan had his copy stashed away, the one he'd stolen once upon a time ago, just waiting for the right opportunity to come along. I thought I could nudge you in the right direction. You wanted to impress me with the film, didn't you? That was your plan? Scare your way into my pants? Hm, how shallow you are, Robert."

"Didn't..."

"Save your last words as they mean nothing to me." A sleek grin spilled across her features. "The only thing I require is what's inside here." She tapped his forehead.

Everything suddenly ached. His arms, legs. Bones. Head. His muscles swelled with pain.

"Now, come on," she said, leaning over him. "Give me a kiss."

She opened her mouth and instead of seeing a tongue, teeth, the hanging pink orb in the back of her throat, he saw nothing but a glowing, white light. A heavenly flash of nothingness. Like staring into a xenon bulb, completely blinding.

She pressed her lips against his and he tasted chaos. Scented ash floating above burning buildings. Sniffed salt in the air over eroding shores. Inhaled smoke over cities on fire.

She tasted like the apocalypse.

And then he experienced the void, that floating black ocean of perpetual nothingness.

ABOUT THE AUTHOR

Tim Meyer dwells in a dark cave near the Jersey Shore. He's an author, husband, father, podcast host, blogger, coffee connoisseur, beer enthusiast, and explorer of worlds. He writes horror, mysteries, science fiction, and thrillers, although he prefers to blur genres and let the stories fall where they may.

You can follow Tim at https://timmeyerwrites.com
OR like his Facebook page here:
www.facebook.com/authortimmeyer

Lightning Source UK Ltd.
Milton Keynes UK
UKHW041203061120
372807UK00003BA/31/J

.

Gallery Books
Editor: Peter Fallon

THE KILLING OF DREAMS

Michael Hartnett

THE
KILLING
OF
DREAMS

Gallery Books

The Killing of Dreams
is first published
simultaneously in paperback
and in a clothbound edition
on 29 May 1992.

The Gallery Press
Loughcrew
Oldcastle
County Meath
Ireland

ISBN 1 85235 086 5 (*paperback*)
   1 85235 087 3 (*clothbound*)

The Gallery Press receives financial assistance from An Chomhairle
Ealaíon / The Arts Council, Ireland.

Contents

PART ONE

Antihex

I thought this war had ended
but it is older than the Cross of Christ
and she is more ancient
than the oldest carving
and still she shines her polished stone
misted with the breathings from her mouth
and spreads infection with fragmented lights.
I will fight her single-handed
and not allow another target in her sights.
I will confine her venom to the south
and make her concentrate on one
to whom a gift was given
which cannot be reduced
and will not bend or give.
A scarcity of victims will produce in her
a spiritual drought:
for even evil dies
and becomes a total negative.
She is a creature beyond grace
who battens on the good.
I will confine her venom to the south.

Orphans

for Angela

The noise that runs across the floor
and takes the wardrobe by the throat
and throws murmurs down the chimney —
this is the wind for her children searching,
the wind searching for her children.
Puffing a gentle shush against the panes
and getting no response
she flings beseeching words
screeching like lost birds
through every crevice
and screams her curses at the slates
and beats her fists upon the buckling gables.
She knows they're captives
in our curtained house,
caught when innocently smelling flowers
or following a butterfly they liked,
and now are lost and ripple lace
upon the tables
and stir with small unnoticed hands
the leaves on potted plants
and sigh from room to room
in this domestic labyrinth of ours.
She pulls her shawl around her in the dark
and leaves the shutters and the windows.
But this is not the end of her attack.
Before the room can draw its breath
and the doors relax she will be back
searching, searching for her children.

Cartomancy

Why does a hearse set out
from that decrepit town
trapped in the hills by history?
Carts with cholera and disease
rumbling down the millstone grit
shoaling through the scanty tar
(that welts and blisters, ambers
in its flattened hide
a Queen Victoria penny
and the thumbprints of a child)
come rumbling still
through superstitious minds,
though now the tar enshrines
continuous pentagrams of tyres
and gravel from the alien plains.
Why *does* the hearse set out?
And changed into the nine of spades
harassed by cardboard queens
it now foretells the past.

The tottering pagodas of my life
deshuffle into cards
and crystal commas sweat along my nose
and deaths and wishes all fan out
on the wrinkled oil-cloth.
The dancing future read in scars
crinkles in the valley of my palm
and sees me running from that past
spilling blood on summer gravel
my split toes poulticed

with a limestone talc.
The oil-lamp in its globe
reflects the drama of the night:
not envisioning too many bright tomorrows
Our Lady of the Sorrows
cowers in her frame;
Father enters from the right,
wonders whether to introduce
a note of fun or fear into the game,
slams enthusiasm like a door,
and the bubble of fine glass
about the wick
crackles into lines like frost,
and as the children's faces try to choose
between fun and fear
indecision shakes the bolt and latch,
and bats like small umbrellas
fold up in the loft
where the bedraggled thatch strokes its many beards.

The Old Lady Says Yes

She is an old woman now
  but still a lady.
All the vulgar versions of her life
  have not changed her;
the crass biographies, the photos
  with ephemeral people,
the murmurings of scandal
  and the hints of evil
crumble into yellow dust
  like the curtains in her window.
In her realm of bric-à-brac
  she receives her children,
even the handicapped, the mad,
  the drunkard in the corner —
none, with their awkward lives
  are welcomed the less warmer —
and if she has many hearts
  not one remains unbroken.
So I come to visit too
  here in her room with my small token
made from the milk that suckled me,
  not chosen just to suit her,
perhaps a bad investment in
  a never-to-happen future.
She puts my verses with her things.
  I have done my duty.

A Falling Out

for Pat Boran

That kind of summer's day when music comes
down from the hills and sings in small back-rooms
and half-sets from a century before
batter their complex hobnails on the floor
and long laments in overcoats and caps
draw tears, reluctant from the porter-taps —
that was the kind of day it was, that day
when I forsook the world of earn and pay.
There, on the cobbles of the market square,
where toothless penny ballads rasped the air,
there among spanners, scollops, hones and pikes,
limp Greyhound cabbage, mending-kits for bikes,
velvet calves in creels, women's overalls,
she shook my hand beside the market stalls.
And there before the coulter of a plough
aware of all the gifts she could endow,
aware, as women are, of all her powers,
as startling as a bunch of winter flowers,
she tricked from me my childish, sacred vow.

I got to know her lovers one by one:
some saw her in an eclipse of the sun,
some saw her practise magic with strange herbs
and made her opaque alchemies of verbs —
some, for her sake, thought blood her favourite wine,
and some thought spirits helped them to divine
her arcane instincts and, as holy fools,
would chant her words not known to any schools.

Some thought that secret nurture made her grow
and more believed she thrived in public show;
some scattered syntax like the blackthorn snow
in flashy spangles on the mud below
and some, like me, immersed themselves in laws,
for what good are the sparks without the straws?
But none of these sufficed. All through the land
I see the poets in their mad distress —
all favoured rivals? No, but victims, yes.
A creature driven by a savage gland,
she takes, and then dismisses, out of hand,
the men and women that she most does bless.
She does not rest, she does not detumesce.

I leave her by a river on a bed,
a silken landscape underneath her head,
and spread her in her finest courting gown
on a spectacular eiderdown
with painted eyes and rings to catch the light
by the oblivious water overnight.
Only the poets can make her come to life,
the stricken catalyst who call her wife —
at dawn I give her bed a gentle shove
and amputate the antennae of love
and watch the river carry her away
into the silence of a senseless bay
where light ignores the facets of her rings
and where names are not the names of things.

PART TWO

Impasse

The students crowd the bar.
In the immense silence of their foreign talk
an occasional noun
flashes across the backdrop of my mind
like a falling star.
I watch them eat *éclairs*,
secure in their own linguistic shells.
(I have poems at hand:
it's words I cannot find.)
I cannot explain my unease
even in my own tongue:
perhaps it's best explained
by my ignorance of theirs.
I can see the poem plain:
it's the words I cannot hear,
as my tongue-tied muses and myself
dumbly regard a poem that waits
for a language to bring it home
to some understanding ear.

Trapped in Shelley

At the end of the page I found myself turning
into a plain that seemed enormous.
The light was dull. I seemed the only occupant.
But two vast and trunkless legs of stone
stood in that desert. Near them on the sand,
half-sunk, a shattered visage lay
like half-burnt blocks in ashes
on a hearth no longer burning.
I was in the wrong place on the wrong errand.
On a pedestal were carved some signs
I could not read nor recognize.
Nothing else was there. Round the decay
of that colossal wreck, boundless and bare,
the lone and level sands stretched far away.
I could not find an exit anywhere.
The visage seemed to watch me where it lay
like broken blocks in ashes
on a hearth no longer burning.
At the edge of the plain I found myself turning.

The Killing of Dreams

They are encoded and are the past,
cannot be implanted in souls or brains,
not by the learning of lists
nor by learning definitions of names:
this is injecting the dream vaccine
which does not make better but makes die
the entities of the mist
that wait in the hollows of our heads.
We graft the cobbled dream
onto the inbuilt dream:
acid on alkali.
Some of us, afraid we lack
the findings of the analyst,
inject the vaccine in
the sanctum of the heart
only to find that it rejects
the artificial part
and leaves us dreamless in the dark.
This, the learning of lists,
this taking water to the well,
this planting of waterweed in streams,
this addiction to the fix
developed by the alchemists of print —
this is the killing of dreams.

Poets Passing

By a perverted act of will
the poet injects limelight in his veins
till what was exhilaration
has become the poet's opium.
Soon in some public place
he must explain and must reshape
the very gift he has
as if the public were the giver,
refine his accent, modify his speech,
must jingle literary cap and bells
and end with insulted brain and liver
far from Wales on a mortuary slab
or with an exhausted heart
in a New York taxi-cab
or out of human reach
in the last of his self-inflicted hells,
by the Mississippi river.

Didactic

1

Language, music, art:
these handmade satellites revolve
in orbit round your head.
You can explode them and explore
the further reaches of inanity instead —
concrete verse and action painting,
all that pyrotechnic razzmatazz;
you can try them all
but you can't escape the facts:
the imagination has no limits.
Art has.

2

It will not fit in the room or the house.
Outside it trundles, knocking over trees
and people, elbowing aside the moon
and tilting Saturn's rings, leaving all
a shambles, plants and stars
and points of mind in chance collisions.
But it can be ordered, broken, in a space
that poets must make in quiet places
or where verses gibe and hector from their shelves;
and then, as if it were a chunk of hill,
it must be tamed by hammerstrokes
and chiselled down to something like an artefact.
And this takes sweat and the most ancient tools of man —

because the dreamer, if he tries to catch
the constellations in his awkward grasp,
just falls asleep before the fire
and lurches through a universe
as shapeless and as fumbling as his gift —
chisel and hammer, against this chunk of hill.
Sweat will find its way to every crease
and even blood: because this rock fights back,
whipping its small stone thorns into the face and chest,
eager for the eyes and belching out a fine
and suffocating dust
to coat the carver and his tools
with blinding atoms of itself.
At last the finished sculpture fills his room;
all living, all domestic chores
revolve around this gleaming stone
which blocks off many doors
and dictates the quality of light
on every shelf and window-ledge;
it is perfect, can express inside its edge
an ordered vision of a certain world;
but the poet has an avid need to act,
to spread the compass of his artefact:
he has to see all thoughts, all acts of humankind
tinged by this petrifaction of his mind
(as artists, after searching, find
a private spectrum to express their schemes —
perhaps of umber, ochre, black:
these colours are the colours of their dreams;
they try to paint the universe with these)
but creation's not amenable to this:
beyond the compass sports and hybrids grow.
Instead he flounders out of bounds,
his panacea mocked by a disease

it was never meant to cure.
Sometimes, with perfect timing, death steps in
and makes the span of living coincide
with the completion of the work on stone,
but, mostly, age insists and the poet cannot see
the very shaping of his chunk of hill
was deed accomplished, mission done.
He never knows that, in the past, he'd won.

Celtic Sacrifice

'Today the people of the gods who came
from the two cold seas still look, perhaps, for blood
(or something subtler, like the impulses
that jump from cell to cell
and make our special universe)
from us, who stole their language,
put it through our spirals and our loops
and have proved, in their staid eyes,
completely irresponsible;
and the price is that our singers
who treat their words like lace
must attend the foreign court
and in due time must be reduced
to miming and die fools.
So instead we send our willing volunteers,
our jugglers, clowns, buffoons,
to cut a caper on the strangers' stage.
But soon the game is up
and they, our poets, must go
to reclaim our honour and to shame
the entertainers and the entertained
and fling a wreath of words well-woven
in the faces of the men of goats and iron.
They die for this, reduced themselves
to jugglers, clowns, buffoons
in the court of the baleful responsible gods.'

Public Art

At least a heap of metal by a wall
sends out some signals:
and rotten timber on a beach
and rusting hulks make homes for shrimps and fleas.
A broken wheel, a length of copper pipe,
their very remnants speak a language;
they are at least a part
of the vocabulary of the tribe.
But this, my sculptor friend,
this borrowing from some theory of some school
is a vision neither theirs nor yours
but stands, a botch of hieroglyphs
the people can't relate to, cannot feel,
detracting from the meaning of the street
and the curving of the hills
with its foreign alphabet of stone and steel.

In the Landscape

1

One more midge in the swirling ghost
that dances like a cone
above a pond with duckweed
spewing from its throat,
I love the tree as much as lightning does;
I care as much for sunset as the sun.

2

Maps tell us nothing.
Marking the position of a well,
the presence of a granite spur,
the distance between monoliths,
they cannot trace
the mental rubrics of the deaths and myths
that occurred here and occur
still in the mindscape of the race
that first enacted rituals
for the spirit of this place.
When the uneasy builders meet
to celebrate an alien laying-on of hands
where their newer churches rise
and they move together in imported stateliness
or in an over-frantic dance,
the old realities among the dancers stand
with sad and comprehending eyes.

Talking Verses

Hey you — 'The Killing of Dreams'!
What's all this stuff about 'vaccines'?
Are you stuck for a trope, or what?
Why not just say that Jung talked rot,
to multiply the dreams we've got
when there's enough to go around?
Come back with me to solid ground.
(I know I'm in another book
but I've come here to take a look
and left my money and my jar
with 'Belladonna at the Bar'
and flexed my stiff iambic wings
just to give a jolt to things
and be more varied in my rhymes
to perpetrate some tasteless crimes
against the so-called holy writ —
though I've another name for it!)
You know this stuff's a load of crap
and if a primping poet adds
another nightmare to his crop —
and other literary fads —
it makes no difference to us
and no one cares a tinker's curse
and no one cares a tinker's fart
whether we are or aren't Art
once we wave the stag-god's antlers
or the old Green Man's acanthus
(it used to be the shepherd's pipes)
or anything that can be found
in *Recommended Archetypes*.

So poem, un-highhorse yourself:
come back with me to solid ground.

This is 'The Killing of Dreams'.
My statement being made,
silence should be my proper stance:
but you have forced me to reply
to your harangue.
You mistake me for some poet's pet,
thrilled, like a critic, at
all the allusions I can get
inside the structure of myself;
but they are not encoded,
these intrusions, they are not the past.
It is just the case
that in this particular place
an accidental language has
me snarled in its hold.
But I am older than all metaphor,
than the oldest epic told,
than this learning of a list,
this defining of a name:
I have survived the tribal scar,
the decorative tattoo.
What I say is what I am
and is not open to tirades from you:
trying not not to be is what I do.

PART THREE

Mountains, Fall on Us

1

White as squid among the roseate prawns
his fingers placed with prim finesse
the seaweed in a green coiffure
about the diamond ice
and gesticulating back he eyed his work
and pursed, 'It's finished; very nice'.
Outside the Easter air was full of drums
and penitents swayed by
with Christs on catafalques
and one man-fearing man at the café door
blew to him a loud and squeaking kiss.
This brought him back to earth,
back to the Confraternity bands
with their jeering trumpets
in the hooded hostile street,
away from his sea mosaics,
away from his rightful place.
With a handkerchief white-winged
like a seagull in his hands
some waiter kindly dabbed
the distraught mascara from his face.

2

At school, in simple linen, whitest cloth,
just twelve, I played a part and played it well.
Away from gaudy pageants, in the cool hall,
away from the drumming in the Easter air,
from satin swamped in crisp cascades of lace,
static in a *tableau*, I was cast
as John, the most beloved disciple.
Ah, no matadors for me,
no heroes of the Civil War —
not even Father, like a flower in steam,
scarlet and saffron in his kitchen whites,
among the copper and the silver pans —
I had a more fatal and more childish dream.
I had found the perfect part
which gave me scope to love and weep
and not to suffer overmuch,
which let me pose, a statue carved from snow
startling in the green palms.
In my fatal, childish dream I could not know
my cross was on its way, already planed
and dovetailed in some workman's hands.

3

I never picture her as young:
always cut from the blackest stone,
the shine of a cross around her neck
as bright as the superstition in her eyes;
and if I say, 'Woman, look at me, your son!'
she looks beyond my shining hair
and ignores the perfume in the room.
She does not see the message in my face;
I'm just, to her, a list of childish woes.
She stores my real sins in dark recesses
with her lace and clothes.
Her mind rejects according to its means
(her mind that dreams the vital dreams
implanted in a body that breaks down
in its faulty universe
and with it breaks her dreams)
a crystal flower growing on a ledge
that always crumbles into dust, and as the ledge
slips down the crystal flower crumbles
and goes down with the débris,
scintillating, faint. She prays for me.
Her milestones are novenas for the dead.

4

In the University Garden, God it all goes wrong —
as I sit here in a soul I do not want,
in a person I can't love,
as by a kiosk students kiss.
I had no real plans when I was young,
just slid into this self I have,
not thinking it would be as bad as this.
Although I cannot live another life —
nor do I want to live the other life —
I live this life which has no joy in it,
no lovers — just accomplices.
I sit, pretend to read, but watch instead
the languorous students in the pampas grass
by the dry fountains, as lovely and as distant as
the poets on their plinths dissolving into sand
in the corrosive smoke.
The flowers are tawdry in the dust
like me, a morning dancer coming home
dishevelled after wine and broken by rebuffs,
my face dissolving like the poets,
the smut of night invading my white cuffs.
I'd love a drink, something cold and nice —
ah yes, the honey of Cuarenta y Tres
jostled by its diamond ice!

5

Oh why do we audition for the glamorous roles
and only get to play the corpse?
I have read the Alexandrian Greek,
his drab epistles to his secret flock
(I vowed my life would be more fine than his,
not the constant victim of some boy
and his battening accomplices).
He found refuge in exotic names,
Dimaratos, Dimitrios, Aimilianos, Manoi,
but his real poems told of real pain.
I vowed my life would be more fine than this.

And now I sit forsaken and stood up
in a no-star eating-house,
a one-armed bandit hurdy-gurdying out
the same synthetic notes,
where the floorboards wear their patina of dirt
as tourists wear a fading tan,
as the overhead electric fan
cuts slices from the curdling smoke
and garlic curses clatter in the kitchens.
Not for me the poet's gold *Dimaratos*
stood up and staring at a plastic rose:
I am living now in one of his more real fictions.

6

So here in this no-star eating-house
I have run out of character:
I am not able for the lines.
This John — if he was beloved —
had in him, by the Cross,
in the copper shadow of the moon's eclipse,
seeds planted that would grow
into a forest of Apocalypse;
nothing in my mind fits me for this part
or for any other; even Judas had his role,
his kiss the pivot of the tale,
he was in the script: no Judas no betrayal;
and Peter destined for his anguish
on the Appian Way
where the guilt broke from his brain
and like a living bead of sweat
jumped from his head and formed a Christ
walking into Rome;
and the good thief on the right (or left) hand
was bound for Paradise
and Pilate shuffled off
to a Roman reprimand.
I am not able for their lines.

7

'There is one left,' the mirror says to me,
as I practise the occupation of the lost,
reading the labels on the shelf.
Behind the bottles' shoulders I can see
my prismatic self.
'But who is left? All the parts are cast,
just a scattering of women on the hill,
Magdalene, the Mother, and the rest:
all the roles are filled.'
'There is one left,' say the ice-cubes in my glass,
chirping from the shaking of my hand,
'he got no promise of eternal bliss,
of green oases flaring in the sand.
He hung on the great loneliness
of his forgotten cross
as the other drifted off to Paradise.
He asked for mercy and was snubbed by Christ.'

I feel the mallets smash my thighs.
I order the cheapest possible cigar.
An alternative saviour joins me at the bar.